EILEEN KNOWLES

ROSES FOR ROBINA

Complete and Unabridged

LINFORD
Leicester

First published in Great Britain in 2005

BROMLEY
PUBLIC
LIBRARIES

AL

CLASS   F

ACC
03087291

UL   INVOICE DATE
       2 6 JAN 2017

First Linford Edition
published 2017

Copyright © 2005 by Eileen Knowles
All rights reserved

A catalogue record for this book is available
from the British Library.

ISBN 978–1–4448–3148–1

Published by
F. A. Thorpe (Publishing)
Anstey, Leicestershire

Set by Words & Graphics Ltd.
Anstey, Leicestershire
Printed and bound in Great Britain by
T. J. International Ltd., Padstow, Cornwall

This book is printed on acid-free paper

Bromley Libraries

3 0128 03087291 8

SPECIAL MESSAGE TO READERS

THE ULVERSCROFT FOUNDATION
(registered UK charity number 264873)

was established in 1972 to provide funds for research, diagnosis and treatment of eye diseases. Examples of major projects funded by the Ulverscroft Foundation are:-

- The Children's Eye Unit at Moorfields Eye Hospital, London
- The Ulverscroft Children's Eye Unit at Great Ormond Street Hospital for Sick Children
- Funding research into eye diseases and treatment at the Department of Ophthalmology, University of Leicester
- The Ulverscroft Vision Research Group, Institute of Child Health
- Twin operating theatres at the Western Ophthalmic Hospital, London
- The Chair of Ophthalmology at the Royal Australian College of Ophthalmologists

You can help further the work of the Foundation by making a donation or leaving a legacy. Every contribution is gratefully received. If you would like to help support the Foundation or require further information, please contact:

THE ULVERSCROFT FOUNDATION
The Green, Bradgate Road, Anstey
Leicester LE7 7FU, England
Tel: (0116) 236 4325

website: www.foundation.ulverscroft.com

ROSES FOR ROBINA

Brett had been the love of Robina's life — until he disappeared without a word. But now he's back in Little Prestbury, to attend his brother's funeral and take on the running of the family estate. And Robbie has to work with him . . . How will her boyfriend Richard react — and how will she cope? Despite telling anyone who'll listen — herself included — that she's over Brett, Robina just can't seem to stop thinking about him . . .

Books by Eileen Knowles
in the Linford Romance Library:

THE ASTOR INHERITANCE
MISTRESS AT THE HALL
ALL FOR JOLIE
HOLLY'S DILEMMA
FORGOTTEN BETROTHAL

1

Robina stared at the drawings spread out on the drawing board, but they made no impression on her. She was too preoccupied by personal problems for them to register. Her boyfriend's mother, Mrs Terrier, was expecting them to visit the following weekend, and Robina was feeling distinctly agitated at the prospect. The visit had been postponed twice already because Richard's mother had felt unwell, which heightened the tension. Robina was expecting the third degree, since it would be the first time they'd met, and she knew in her heart of hearts that no girlfriend was ever going to pass as a suitable future daughter-in-law to the redoubtable Mrs Terrier.

'So what,' said Robina out loud, and sighed. Even though she had stressed many times to herself it was Richard she was considering marrying and not his mother, she knew that wasn't strictly true. Richard, so gentle and considerate, unstintingly gave his mother the benefit of the doubt and loyally sacrificed much of his spare time to her well-being. Still, that was only one of her problems. The next, and far more worrying, was the imminent prospect of meeting her ex-fiancé. It would be four years since she had last seen Brett, and now — just when she was contemplating a lasting relationship with Richard — he had to reappear on the scene. Brett was her past — over and forgotten, so she didn't welcome it being revived — and yet . . .

With a desperate sigh she settled down to peruse her work. Brett Scott could be married with children by now — what did she care! If she didn't get started on the detail drawings, she was going to be late for her date with Richard. He never made a fuss, but would more than likely say she worked too hard, making her feel guilty for time spent daydreaming.

A short while later, her younger sister burst into the office like a human tornado. 'He's back!' she shrieked, eager to impart her earth-shattering news.

'So?' Robina remarked sourly, momentarily distracted away from the computer screen by the draught from the door.

'How do you know who I mean? I never said.'

'Huh. Brett Scott, of course. Who else would drive a Ferrari in this locality?'

'Gosh! Has he really got a Ferrari? I didn't know. I've just been talking to Georgie on the telephone, but she didn't say anything about the car. What's it like?'

'Bright red and expensive-looking. What do you expect?'

Susan pulled a face and plumped herself down on the edge of the desk, carelessly crumpling some paperwork.

'He must have made a fortune while he's been away then. I wonder if he'll be staying on after the funeral? I wonder if . . . '

'I haven't a clue, Susie. Now, please will you leave and let me get on with these drawings?' Robina rescued the papers and smoothed them out somewhat irritably. She scowled at her sister. 'I need to concentrate. I haven't time for tittle-tattle right now. Go and find someone else to confide in.'

'OK, Robbie. Sorry, I'm sure, but I thought you'd want to know he was back in circulation. After all . . . '

'Susie! I neither know nor care about Brett Scott any more. He can go to hell for all I'm concerned.'

Susan slithered off the desk and flounced out, miffed by her sister's response. Robina stared blindly at the computer screen. Why couldn't he have stayed out of her life? Why did he have to return now, upsetting her erstwhile placid existence? Instinct had made her look out of the window on hearing the

4

ominous sound of a powerful car changing gear at the crossroads. The flagrantly conspicuous car flashed past the works entrance, and she had known immediately to whom it belonged. The prodigal son had returned.

He wouldn't think to come home inconspicuously after dark; oh no, he had to announce quite openly he was back. *Brazen*, her father would call it. He had to return for the funeral, obviously — Marcus had been his brother, after all — but then what? Returning to the work at hand, she scanned the drawing spread out beside her, then picked up a pencil and tried to concentrate on some calculations. She settled to work with determined diligence, pensively flicking her hair back out of her eyes. It was a gesture that all who knew her regarded as a signal to leave her be.

Her father poked his head round the door. 'Any messages, love?'

'No, Dad. All quiet, I'm afraid.'

'I'm off to Pearson's, then. I hope to

be back by lunchtime, all being well.' Taking off his hard hat and overalls, he retrieved a coat from the peg inside the door.

'OK, Dad. Mind how you go, and the best of luck.'

'Thanks. I'll need it, but it will be a worthwhile little job if we can get it.'

They could certainly do with the contract because business had been rather slack of late. They didn't like having to lay off any of the men — but if things didn't improve soon, they might have to, Robina thought grimly. Pushing her hair back off her face again, she frowned at the drawing on the screen, determined to finish it before lunch. She knew the work was needed rather urgently, but her father wouldn't pressurise her for it. Accuracy was needed more than speed at this stage.

At one o'clock, she ran off the last drawing print ready to issue to the works, and sat back with a stretch and a yawn. Switching on the kettle, she paused to look in the small mirror hanging on the wall of what constituted a cloakroom. *Would Brett notice any difference?* she wondered, running slender, ringless fingers through her shoulder-length hair. *Maybe I should get my hair cut*, she thought. *Surprise Richard with a new hairstyle.* Twirling blonde curls up on top of her head, she grimaced, and decided she hadn't changed much in looks since Brett's speedy departure. But being jilted had certainly left its mark in other ways. She lost weight almost overnight, and now maintained her slim figure without dieting. And her eyes were lacklustre in comparison to how they used to be. Brett used to call them sparkling sapphires and tease her about their worth, saying he couldn't afford them.

'Why is it, no matter what I do, it always come back to Brett Scott?' she fumed to herself, and settled down with her tea and sandwiches, ruminating over what she was going to do when they met. The village was only small, so they couldn't avoid each other, and she wanted to be ready for him. She knew it was going to be a difficult first meeting. She mulled over what had happened. Was the gossip going to start up again? She hoped not, for her parents' sake as well as her own. They had been marvellously supportive at the time, but she didn't want them to have to go through it again, especially now when business wasn't too rosy. They had enough to worry about.

For the rest of the day Robina concentrated on her work, double-checking everything because she knew that with lack of concentration, costly errors could often be made, and that was the last thing they needed. Her father reappeared during the afternoon, rather later than expected, but jubilantly waving a bunch of papers.

'We've got it. Pearson has screwed us down with the price, but I think we can just about live with it. It will mean we have work to keep us going for another couple of months at least.'

'That's marvellous,' Robina greeted him warmly. 'How did you manage it? I thought we would be beaten on delivery, or are you expecting me to be working all hours to get the drawings done in time?' Robina looked anxiously at her father as he plonked the papers on the desk, and only narrowly missed sweeping her calculator on to the floor.

'I'll give you a hand, and you know we did need the work,' he wheedled.

'How long have we got?' she asked with alarm. She knew Pearson's always expected a very quick turnaround, although to give them credit they did pay promptly.

'Oh, plenty of time. It's fairly straightforward. Don't worry, we'll manage — we always do, don't we?' Her father put his arm round her shoulders to give her a reassuring squeeze. 'If necessary, we'll get Jim in to give us a hand.'

When he left, Robina finished what she was doing, and then spread out the design drawings for the Pearson job on the plan chest, trying to assess how much time she would need to detail it. She looked for likely tricky areas which could be time-consuming to resolve, and had to agree it was work they could well do with, even if it meant her spending some time during the evenings working on it. It looked reasonably straightforward, so maybe her father was right. She hoped so. Occasionally, when they had too much work for her to cope with, they employed another draughtsman who did work in his spare time at home. She'd heard Jim had recently been made redundant, so he would probably be available if required.

Robina arrived home, and as she hung up her coat, she overheard the family chatting in the living room. The conversation was inevitably about Brett, so she paused momentarily to listen.

'The talk in the village is that he's looking extremely prosperous,' her mother remarked, 'but they also say he's aged quite a lot. No-one seems to know where he's been or what he's been doing.'

'Got a cheek coming back at all.' That was her father sounding gruff with annoyance. 'I hope he doesn't stay long, that's all I can say.'

'Must be wealthy to own a Ferrari,' Susie gushed. 'I can't wait to see it. I wonder if he'll give me a ride in it? I've never . . . '

'Came on his own?' her father asked, cutting his younger daughter off short.

'I believe so,' his wife replied. 'No sign of a wife, but that doesn't mean . . . '

Robina entered the room, trying desperately hard to look indifferent and unconcerned.

'The funeral's tomorrow,' her father said, including her in the conversation. 'I reckon we should go as a united family. What do you say, Robbie?'

Robina swallowed hard. She knew she was going to have to meet Brett one day, but she wasn't ready yet — she hadn't got her emotions under control.

11

'You could represent the firm and the family, couldn't you? Someone ought to man the telephone, and I have plenty of work I should be doing.'

'No, Robbie, I think it would be only fitting for us to go together as a family on this occasion,' her father said, gently but firmly. 'It's what would be expected, you know. It might be easier on you in the long run, too.'

'I suppose so,' she agreed reluctantly. There wasn't much point in arguing; she may as well accept the fact gracefully and steel herself to remain calm. It would be the first hurdle over with, and she thought if she could get through that she could cope with anything.

'Do I have to go too?' asked her younger sister, pulling a face. 'I was going to go swimming with Georgie. It's all arranged.'

'You are going to go and show some respect, young lady,' admonished her mother. 'You can go swimming some other time. You'd best go and ring

12

Georgina now and explain.'

'Oh poo,' said Susan, flouncing out of the room in a huff. 'Nobody would miss me. I don't see why I should have to go to some stuffy funeral. I don't work for the Scotts, and he wasn't my boyfriend or anything.'

Robina flinched.

'You'll have to meet him sometime, Robbie love,' said her father, giving her a commiserating look. 'May as well be at the funeral as anywhere, and get it over with.'

'I know, Dad, don't worry. I *am* over him. After all, it was four years ago. Time heals, as they say. Nothing he says or does is of the slightest interest to me.'

'Yes, I know, lass, but it will still be a mite difficult for you meeting again for the first time, so it may as well be in a crowd. You know the whole village will probably turn out to pay their respects, so it would look odd if we didn't do the same. Marcus was a decent bloke, and it's him we are paying our respects to.'

Robina slept badly, tossing and turning as she mentally prepared herself for the ordeal the next day. She kept going over and over the anguish she'd gone through with when she learned of Brett's unexpected departure, and the despair when she didn't hear from him. She still found it hard to believe he could do it to her.

The funeral was taking place at eleven o'clock. The sun shone brilliantly as the Davison family walked the short distance to the church at the end of the village main street. It somehow seemed incongruous to be attending a sad event on such a beautiful day. Clumps of daffodils bordered the path, cheerfully adding their own brand of mockery to the occasion. It was April, spring was in the air, and a new beginning was anticipated — with Richard. Maybe after the weekend, with the visit to Brighton behind them, they could start making plans for their future.

Nearly every pew in the tiny church was occupied. Robina felt all eyes were on her as she walked in with her family. They were all smirking behind their hands, she thought, remembering how the Scott family had humiliated her. She could sense what they were all thinking, and held her head even higher, refusing to let them see how much it still hurt. She knew they had all thought it strange that Brett had chosen her to go out with, and her he'd asked to marry.

She still occasionally took out his ring and tried it on in the privacy of her room, recalling the treasured moment Brett had presented it to her. He had gone down on one knee in the time-honoured fashion, and she had accepted with such joy. It was a beautiful ring, given with enduring love — or so she'd thought at the time. How wrong she had been! Brett's rejection had been so unforeseen and cruel that she wondered at the time if she would ever get over it. It had been months before she could bring herself to accept he had really deserted her. Finally, she'd immersed herself in work to blot out her misery when all the excuses she could think of led to nothing.

Today, she wore a smart navy-blue outfit trimmed in white, and as a concession for the occasion, a small navy hat perched on the back of her head. She felt self-conscious wearing it, little realising how sweet and attractive she looked with her hair swept up in a neat chignon and the tailored suit showing off her trim figure. She seemed totally unaware of any admiring glances she received from the male members of the congregation.

The Davison family located a pew near the rear of the church, and Robina found herself, by some unhappy coincidence, on the end nearest the aisle. The church was packed; it seemed as if the whole village had turned out, just as her father predicted. After all, thought Robina, most of them owed their livelihood to the Scotts in one form or another, even if they didn't directly employ them. They had many tenant farmers as well as employees working in the forestry, the timber yard, the farm and the gardens. They would all be there, wondering what the future held for them. Would their jobs and livelihoods be safe?

The organist played solemn incidental music, and then Robina felt the hairs on the back of her neck prickle. Despite the unseasonably warm weather, she shivered. The cortege was entering the rear porch. He'd arrived! She just knew Brett had arrived. Keeping her eyes firmly fixed on a woman's hat in the pew in front, she held her breath, knowing he must pass within touching distance. She wouldn't look. She should be reading the order of service and finding the hymns.

It seemed to take an age before the family members drew level with her. Slowly, the procession moved up the aisle, and her eyes automatically wavered left to catch the first glimpse of her ex-fiancé. His grief-stricken parents seemed to have aged overnight, Robina thought as they went by. She knew they weren't much older than her own mum and dad, but they looked much older now in mourning. Then came Brett accompanying his younger sister, bleakly keeping his eyes averted.

Despite her resolve not to, she couldn't help looking at him. She didn't know quite what she expected to see, but his appearance shocked her. He was nothing like the Brett she knew — the Brett she remembered. It wasn't just the sadness of the occasion — that, she could accept — but he looked so much older; he even had grey flecks in his dark hair. And where were the curls? It was now cut so short — so staid and businesslike.

Robina remembered little of the service; her mind was occupied elsewhere. It came as quite a surprise to find it was all over, and the bereaved family were once again making their way down the aisle. As Brett passed the pew where she waited, his dark eyes stared directly at her, probing in their intensity in a sad, almost apologetic way. She sensed despair and anguish in his heart, but she didn't think it was only because of Marcus.

At the door as they filed out, she managed to shake hands and mutter her condolences in a calm voice that sounded foreign to her ears. It didn't appear to be real. It wasn't happening. It was if she was watching from the sidelines as the real Robina Davison reacted to the circumstances in a cold, apathetic way. Brett was a stranger to her.

'It was good of you to come,' he said in a tight, subdued voice, holding her hand slightly longer than necessary. 'I'm sorry we had to meet again like this.'

2

The next morning, as she worked at the computer, the door opened, but Robina was so engrossed in what she was doing that she didn't turn round immediately. She wanted to complete the change she was making while she remembered it. The men from the works often popped in to query something on a drawing, and she assumed that was who it was this time.

It was only when she heard the well-remembered, seductive voice calling her name that she realised just who the visitor was. It had been four years since anyone had called her by that name. Nobody ever called her Rosaline these days if they knew what was good for them — or, rather, Rosie, the shortened version that he always used. Not many people knew her full name of Robina Rosaline Davison. The blood

20

drained from her face as she spun round in her chair to face him.

'You! What are you doing here? What do you want?' She glared at him, her eyes flashing with anger, shock and pure astonishment. She did want to see him alone, but not here — not now, she wasn't ready. It was too soon. She wasn't prepared. He must have walked, she thought inconsequentially, because she hadn't heard the car. At least to that extent he had been discreet. Not that it really mattered one way or the other. 'Why have you come here?'

'To see you, of course, Rosie,' he said softly. 'You must have known I would. You were expecting me, weren't you?'

Framed in the doorway, he almost filled the opening. Gone was the dark suit of yesterday, and in its place were a pale blue roll-necked jumper and slim-fitting slacks that only served to accentuate his splendid, muscular physique. He'd always been broad-shouldered and well-developed, but now he appeared much leaner, yet fitter. His face still bore the ravaged look of the previous day, even as he smiled in greeting. It was a wary smile, though, as if unsure of his welcome — as indeed he might be. Previously, he would have made some light-hearted joke to make her laugh, but not this time. This was a much more serious Brett. This was a man who could walk out of her life without a word of apology or explanation. A man who captured her heart and promised he would be hers for life, only to desert her within a matter of days. Did he really think he could waltz back as if the last four years had never happened, and pick up where he left off?

She could feel his dark, honey-brown eyes appraising her, and felt herself blush at his intense scrutiny. Seated at the desk, her skirt had ridden up, and she realised that she was displaying a considerable amount of leg, which she tried now to surreptitiously hide. She breathed in deeply in order to recover some composure, wishing that she had worn slacks that day as she quite often did.

'Yes, I suppose so,' she said coldly. 'Won't you come in and take a seat? I had better remember my manners. At least *I* know how to behave!' She hadn't expected him to come calling at the office, and it hardly seemed an appropriate place for an argument.

'How are you?' he asked, ignoring the offer of a chair. Closing the door, he leaned back nonchalantly against it, his eyes never leaving her face. Robina wasn't taken in by his apparent self-restraint, though; she sensed his unease. 'You're looking well, Rosie. You've changed from a delectable teenager into a rather beautiful young woman, I see.'

She winced. 'I've grown up, if that is what you mean. I had to, and I learned the hard way, if you remember,' she snapped back at him, gripping the chair arms in an attempt to control her feelings. Being alone with him in the

23

small office was much more difficult to cope with than she had ever anticipated, and she was glad she was sitting down, because she had the feeling that her legs would not support her at that precise moment.

'I'm sorry, Rosie.'

'Don't call me that. I hate it.'

'I really am truly sorry, Robbie. I know I hurt you . . . '

'Huh! Leaving me to face the music, you just packed up and left, you miserable so-and-so,' she snorted angrily. All the anger that had been building over the last few days surfaced. All the hurt she felt all those years ago at his desertion welled up in her, and she let fly. 'Left it to your parents to ring me to say that you had gone abroad. *Urgent family business,* they said! As if I believed them! All I got from you was a lousy postcard several months later. You really take some beating if you think you can come back and expect me to smile and say, 'All is forgiven, Brett.

Welcome home.' As far as I'm concerned, you are history. I learned my lesson well. You'll not make a fool of me a second time, Brett Scott. I'm twenty-one now, not a simpering seventeen-year-old.'

'I'm sorry,' he said bleakly, running a hand through his short-cropped hair. 'I'd like to explain, and I will, I promise, but now isn't the time. Please take my word for it that you were better off without me.'

'You're damned right, I *am* better off without you. I don't care any more, so you can forget your excuses; I have no wish to hear them. It's too late for that. Just go, and leave me alone. I never want to see you again,' she cried, her hands clenched desperately as she struggled with her muddled emotions. 'Just stay away from me, do you hear? Stay out of my life.'

He seemed shocked by her outburst and fixed his gaze on her hands. 'Not married yet, I see — any boyfriend on the horizon?' he asked tautly.

'Of course. Did you expect me to stay at home knitting or twiddling my thumbs all this time? You might think you are God's gift to women, but no man is indispensable — not even you, Brett. You taught me a valuable lesson that has stood me in good stead — not to put my trust in the male of the species too readily. Now, if you don't mind, I have work to do that requires complete concentration, so I'd be obliged if you would leave. We have nothing more to say to each other.'

She couldn't bear for him to see how his reappearance had made her reel with dismay. She only hoped the telephone didn't ring because she was too choked up to answer it.

'Yes, I can see how it is, so I won't keep you. I never meant things to turn out like this, please believe that. Maybe one day . . . ' he began, and then thought better of it. 'Give my regards to your family. I'll try to keep out of your way as much as possible, but you must know that in a small place like this, some meetings will be unavoidable. I'm not sure how long I'll be staying. It rather depends . . . ' Sadly, he turned and walked out, his shoulders hunched with dejection. 'See you around,' he called over his shoulder.

Robina stared after him in total turmoil, her eyes stinging with unshed tears. She'd noted the tired lines round his eyes; they seemed to have lost their old mischievous gleam, but that was to be expected, having just lost his brother. He hadn't looked at all the cheerful, happy person she had known and loved. He looked careworn, and much older than his thirty years, she thought, despite the weather-beaten appearance. The touch of grey showing in his thick, dark hair added to his attraction in some strange way, but his face, chiselled too thin, made him look gaunt and harassed. Whatever he'd been doing these past four years hadn't been all pleasure by the look of him.

For the rest of the day, Robina closed her mind to the outside world and worked on the drawings. It was difficult, but not impossible, and when her father arrived at five o'clock she was still furiously beavering away. It was the only way she could cope, just as it had been four years ago. It was like putting up the shutters on everything away from the computer screen.

'Time to call it a day, love,' he said, dropping on to a chair by the desk with a deep sigh. 'It's been quite a day. How's tricks? Think you can have those drawings for the men tomorrow?'

He looked tired, she thought, mostly due to the anxiety about lack of orders and work for the men. She knew he worried if he had to lay them off for a while, thinking about their families and how they would cope. At least they had the Pearson job to get on with now.

'I've nearly finished. I must just do this, though, while I remember it. You go on, Dad; I'll be home directly.'

'Well, don't be too long or you'll have your mother after you. She already thinks I'm a slave-driver where you're concerned. You're overdue for a holiday, she keeps reminding me.' He got wearily to his feet and went out shaking his head wryly. He knew how hard it had been for his daughter, attending the funeral and meeting Brett again with all the villagers present. He felt proud of the way she had handled it, but knew better than to tell her so. She was a chip off the old block: so steady, sensible and reliable!

★ ★ ★

After the meal, Robina helped her mother with the dishes while Susan was delegated to feed the cat.

'Didn't Mrs Scott wear a funny hat at the funeral?' Susan said, reaching for the milk jug. 'She might well have got it from an Oxfam shop or a jumble sale. Brett looked gorgeous as ever, though, didn't he just?' she added dreamily. 'So tall, dark and handsome, like a true romantic hero coming to the rescue of the family fortunes, only in a Ferrari instead of on his trusty steed,' she tittered. 'It's a super car. I'll bet it does a hundred easily. All the girls in the village are laying bets on who will be the first to have a ride in it.'

'Susan, go to your room if that is the best you can do,' her mother chastised her sharply. 'Have you no sensitivity? Don't you realise how you are upsetting Robbie? For goodness' sake, child, when will you ever grow up?'

'I'm sorry, I didn't think. Sorry, Rob.' She skulked away. 'You said you didn't care any more. I didn't mean anything.'

'I despair of that girl sometimes,' her mother went on. 'She's not at all like you were at her age, Robbie. I don't know where she gets it from.'

'Give her time, Mother; after all, she is only seventeen. It's a difficult age, as I remember.'

'She's nearly eighteen. Time she learned some discretion! But she was right, though, that hat did look rather dreadful,' her mother remarked. 'The Scotts looked devastated. I wonder what they will do now? Maybe they'll sell up and retire once they've got Juliet off their hands, do you think?'

'It has hit them rather hard. They thought the world of Marcus — I think he was their favourite son. I never could understand why, because he was always the more serious one of the two. He hardly ever smiled that I noticed. He was a good estate manager, though, I suppose,' said Robina solemnly, 'and Brett will have his work cut out trying to emulate him.'

'Brett is back for good, then, do you think?' asked her mother cautiously.

'Yes, I guess he is,' Robina said, summoning up all her willpower to reply calmly. 'He called at the works to see me this morning.'

Her mother, recognising the signs of tension, quickly changed the subject and asked if she was going out with Richard that evening.

'No, I'll go back to the office for a little while, as I've something I want to finish off for tomorrow.'

After Robina left the kitchen, her mother sat down in the rocking chair and sighed. She hoped that Brett's return wasn't going to upset Robina enough for her to want to leave Little Prestbury. Would she leap into marrying Richard before she was satisfied he was the right man for her? She hoped not. Richard was all right in his way, but perhaps too conventional and staid. Still, it was for Robbie to decide.

Life was fraught enough at the moment, what with Susan's exams and possible university place, plus worrying about the works and how hard it had been financially for some time now . . . She gently rocked to and fro until she felt calmer. Whatever Robina wanted to do, she would accept, because she knew her eldest daughter wasn't one to do anything without a great deal of thought — not like Susan, who was so mercurial and unpredictable. Talk about chalk and cheese!

★ ★ ★

Richard arrived early on the Saturday morning. He smiled brightly. 'All ready, I see,' he said as Robina handed him her overnight case.

'How is your mother?' Robina asked, rather hoping that the visit could be postponed yet again.

'Fine,' came the reply. 'I rang her before I set off, and she sounded chirpy and looking forward to seeing us.'

Robina took her place in the passenger seat and murmured, 'How nice.'

'I said we'd stop for lunch on the way, so we should be there by about two o'clock. It will save Mother extra work, and it means we can make it a leisurely trip.'

Robina settled back, determined to enjoy the weekend. The weather was fine and dry and the scenery pleasant. Richard was an interesting companion and it felt good to be away from the village for a while. For a few hours at least she could forget about a certain individual who seemed to dominate her

33

thoughts far too readily. Brett's presence in the village bothered her more than she cared to admit. She firmly put any thoughts of Brett to the back of her mind, and concentrated on Richard. He was being his usual charming self, eager to please, and obviously anxious about introducing her to his mother. She tried her best to reassure him that everything would be fine, although she herself was having reservations.

At two o'clock precisely, they pulled up in front of a neat detached bungalow in a quiet cul-de-sac in the better part of the town. The garden was immaculate, with daffodils and tulips standing to attention in regimented rows beside the path. The grass was smooth as a billiards table, the edges trimmed to perfection. Robina smiled grimly to herself and watched the net curtains, wondering if even now she was being inspected. The door opened as they approached, and a tall, gaunt woman appeared.

'Hello, Mother,' Richard hailed her,

and with his arm round Robina propelled her forward. 'It's time you met Robbie.'

'How do you do,' his mother said, and Robina wondered if she should shake her hand or even curtsey. She was saved the embarrassment of having to decide as Mrs Terrier retreated into the hallway.

'We'll fetch the bags later. Have you put the kettle on?' Richard sounded full of bonhomie. 'We didn't want to be late, but we are gasping for a cuppa, and I've been telling Robbie about your wonderful Dundee cake. I hope you've made some.'

His mother smiled briefly. 'Won't you show Robina into the sitting room, and I'll bring you some refreshments.'

Robina chewed her lip. Mrs Terrier was so formal, and judging by what she had seen so far, she was extremely house-proud. There wasn't a speck of dust anywhere. The sitting room was austere, with cold leather chairs and a serviceable patterned carpet of dull brown. There were no plants or pictures to relieve the gloomy decor. Robina shuddered inwardly.

★ ★ ★

Three hours later, they were walking hand-in-hand along the seafront, breathing in some fresh ozone. 'What do you think of Brighton, then, Robbie?' Richard asked. They were meandering slowly back to the house having seen the sights. Mrs Terrier had urged them to go before the rain came, and Robina was pleased to do so. The meeting with Richard's mother had been as daunting as she had expected, and she was wondering how they were going to cope with the rest of the time they felt obliged to stay.

'Fine!' She grinned and pecked his cheek. He was probably as uncomfortable as she was. 'Great place to spend a week's holiday, I imagine.'

Richard paused and stared out to sea. 'Something wrong?' Robina asked.

36

She knew he didn't like public displays of emotion, but it was only a kiss, for heaven's sake.

'No.' He shook his head and set off to walk again.

She had the feeling something was amiss, but she hadn't a clue what it could be. The bombshell came after dinner. Mrs Terrier sat in her usual chair, and Robina chose to sit on the settee so that Richard could sit beside her. She had the feeling that his mother had something in her mind that she was about to reveal. Whatever was about to be discussed, she felt certain it was not going to be to her liking. She couldn't put her finger on it, but she had the distinct impression that she was being lined up by the pair of them for some momentous news.

'Now that Richard is likely to be transferring back to Brighton, I thought you should . . . '

Robina gasped out loud.

'Didn't you know, my dear?' his

mother said, with what Robina saw as a satisfied smile.

Richard gave a monumental sigh and stared at his feet.

'Why didn't you tell me?' Robina asked, biting back words of anger.

'It isn't definite . . . I haven't decided . . . I only learned about it myself the other day.' He frowned across at his mother. 'How did you know?'

'Now that your firm has been taken over and its branch closures were announced, I made it my business to find out. Anyway, that is beside the point. What I was about to tell you is, the next-door bungalow is about to be put on the market, and I immediately thought how convenient it would be.'

Mrs Terrier waffled on about how his father would have approved and how practical it would be, but Robina gave up listening. She could see it all so clearly, Richard would be drawn into his mother's web with no escape, and she was expected to be jumping for joy. It sounded cut and dried.

'I'm sorry,' Richard murmured, and gave her hand a squeeze, clearly shaken. Out loud, he said, 'Mother, it's too early to be discussing such things. I've told you before, I have no desire to return to live here. Besides, I have to consider Robina's wishes. She may not want to . . .'

His mother shrugged her shoulders. She slowly got to her feet and made for the door. 'I'm off to bed. I feel a headache coming on.'

She wasn't the only one, thought Robina grimly.

'I think I'll turn in too,' she said coldly. For two pins she would have walked out. Richard had been evasive — asking about her views on Brighton, showing her the sights, pretending they were holidaymakers. All the time, he was lining her up for the unpalatable truth.

'I'm sorry,' Richard said, trying to pull her into his arms.

Robina moved away.

'Honestly, Robbie, I never told her

anything — about us — about the job. She must have been speaking to my boss, who unfortunately happens to be a friend of Dad's. I wouldn't do anything without consulting you, sweetheart.'

Robina chewed her lip. 'Would you seriously consider your mother's suggestion? Do you really want to live next door? I know it's kind of her to help with the purchase, but . . . '

'I really don't know. The other option is to accept voluntary redundancy, but I'm none too happy about that. There's so much to think about. Us, for example. Are you ready to make our engagement official?'

Robina shook her head. 'I'm sorry, Richard, but in view of the latest information I need more time. You do understand, don't you?'

3

'I hear he's been out in Australia — sheep-farming.'

'I heard it was America. I can't see him as a sheep farmer.'

'No, I have it on good authority that he's been living it up on the French Riviera. He inherited a fortune and went to sow a few wild oats.'

'That sounds more than probable. He's obviously not short of a bob or two. Got quite a tan, too. Wonder if he's married?'

'That car must have set him back a tidy sum. Came alone didn't he?'

'Not heard of any woman in tow.'

Robina heard the rumours about Brett, but made no comment. She didn't care where he'd come from or what he'd been doing these past four years. She didn't care whether he was married or not — or so she tried to tell herself. She just wished he would go away and never come back.

She was jumpy, nervous, and upset by her muddled emotions. Ever since the visit to Brighton, she had been dispirited. She knew there was no way she would go and live so close to his mother, so it rather looked as if she wouldn't be marrying Richard after all. Their first argument was on the way home, when he seemed to be agreeing with his mother that it was a sensible arrangement she was proposing. Robina couldn't believe her ears, and snapped that it was time he grew up and saw how his mother was manipulating him.

In the end, they agreed to let things lie for a while, since his move to Brighton wasn't confirmed. As they parted, Richard said, 'It isn't easy, you know. I am the only kin Mother has left. I know she appears to be a hypochondriac, and overbearing at times, but ... well ... she is my mother.'

* * *

In the post one morning, there was a letter — or, rather, an instruction — from the Prestbury Grange Estate Office. Would Robina make an appointment with Brett, as he had some work he had to discuss with her? She had been wondering when they would hear about the project Marcus had instigated shortly before he'd been killed. She wished now that they hadn't taken on the job, but they had already agreed to do it, so there was nothing else for it but to grit her teeth and follow it up.

When she felt she had herself under some sort of control, she rang the Estate Office number, hoping by some miracle it wasn't Brett that answered. She'd had no problem dealing with Marcus on a business level, but she knew that coping with Brett was going to be a different kettle of fish altogether. It was going to be impossible to keep feelings out of it.

'I gather you have some work of

interest to Davison Fabrications? I suppose it's to do with the Hay Lane site?' she said briskly, shocked by the effect his voice had on her.

'That's right, Robbie. When could you come to see me?'

'My father could call on you later this morning if it's urgent.'

'No, Robbie. Don't misunderstand me. I wish to see you.'

'Why . . . me?' she said, annoyed to find herself stammering like an adolescent schoolgirl. 'My father deals with that side of the business,' she added, rather untruthfully. The last thing she wanted now was to see Brett alone, especially at the Grange. Since his return to Little Prestbury, she had managed to remain quietly composed in front of others, and was gradually accepting the situation, although not happy about it. Every time she heard his car go past the works, she leapt to her feet to catch a glimpse of him. It was a kind of torment she went through, not wanting to actually meet him and yet desperate to see him. She found herself comparing him with Richard, and concluding that any thoughts of marrying Richard were not viable. She knew she wasn't making sense, but only hoped nobody else saw her bewilderment.

'I need your expertise,' Brett answered blandly. 'I suppose I could always go elsewhere, but I prefer dealing locally if I can, and I have heard nothing but good reports about your firm — and you in particular.'

She knew for the sake of her father and the firm that she would have to go, however reluctant she might feel about it, so she gave in. He must know that they needed work to keep the men employed, and she couldn't let the firm down. News like that spread quickly through the community.

'What time would be convenient?' she said with a resigned sigh.

'We could discuss it over dinner, if you prefer it?' he said softly; wistfully, she thought.

'No,' she almost shouted. 'I prefer to do business during office hours. I'll come up after lunch — say, two o'clock.'

She remembered the Estate Office as being Marcus's domain. He'd always intimidated her, Brett's older brother. He'd made her feel so immature, and at the time seemed to scorn her adoration of his brother. Looking back, she realised that Marcus was simply older, with all the responsibility of running the estate, which left him little time to be frivolous like Brett. In those days she had idolised Brett, agreed with anything he said, done anything he wanted. He was her hero stepped right out of a romantic novel, with his dashing good looks and beguiling sense of humour, and the son of the local magnate — what more could she have asked for?

On one occasion, Brett had taken her into the office and Marcus had discovered them there. They had only gone in to shelter from a sudden passing shower, but had started kissing and cuddling. Marcus, entering unexpectedly, had given them a thoroughly disgusted look before storming out without saying a word. Robina had felt terribly embarrassed, but Brett had grinned and said he was probably jealous.

During the rest of the morning, Robina dealt with mundane paperwork. She was in no mood to go back to the computer. She had to make three attempts at typing out an invoice before she was happy with it, her fingers just wouldn't co-operate in finding the correct keys, and she was a perfectionist when it came to sending out letters, etc.

She made herself eat lunch, although her stomach rebelled at the thought of food, and soon after half-past one she set off for her appointment, having told her father earlier where she was going so he could answer the phone in her absence. He had been preoccupied, and had merely acknowledged the prospect of another job and wished her luck.

Robina decided to walk because it

gave her time to think. She had always enjoyed strolling through the Grange's land accompanied by Brett and the dogs. Today, though, it was a mistake. She could see that now as she hurried along the path towards the Estate Office; it evoked too many happy memories that she had being trying to forget. The rhododendron shrubbery where they once hid away from prying eyes, and the path leading off through the woods where they strolled so often in an evening . . . It all came flooding back as she pressed on, blinking back the tears.

'Damn, damn, damn,' she scolded herself, painfully aware of her resolve crumbling. She should have insisted that he deal with her father.

Brett must have been watching for her, because he opened the door before she even knocked. Greeting her warily, he bade her enter with utmost courtesy.

'I see you walked. Would you care for some coffee?'

'No thanks, I'd like to get down to

business. I have a lot of work to get on with,' she said frostily.

'Yes, of course, Ros- . . . Robbie. Just as you wish. I know this is difficult for you, just as it is for me, so I'll make it brief. Come and sit down while I explain the changes I have in mind.'

Robina found herself facing Brett across the desk littered with papers and sketches. She deliberately tried to keep to a professional approach and remained coldly aloof, even though her stomach was tied up in knots. She steeled herself to remain unaffected by him. His smile was so disarming and familiar that she had to bite her lip hard to stop the tears forming again.

He fidgeted with the papers, shuffling them about nervously as if avoiding having to look at her. He was tense. It was true — she wasn't the only one finding the situation difficult, it would appear. What a pity Davison Fabrications had already tendered for the job, which was why he probably felt he had to pursue it with them when he would much rather have gone elsewhere, given their particular circumstances.

Maybe she should say they were now too busy and let him off the hook. She felt certain her father would understand if she withdrew their tender. He had been prepared to work for Marcus, because they had no quarrel with him, but Brett was different. After the shabby way he had treated her, both her parents felt it inappropriate to have anything more to do with him. Recently, the Davison involvement with the Prestbury Estate was on a purely business footing, and had been fairly remunerative. It would be a shame to lose the custom, but on the other hand . . .

Brett coughed and cleared his throat. 'I gather you are involved in Marcus's scheme to convert the old barn down Hay Lane into self-contained units?' He became brusquely businesslike.

'Yes, that's correct,' Robina replied, bringing her mind sharply back to focus on the job in question. This was a new, different Brett. He was the businessman, the client, and the manager of a large, extensive concern, not her sweetheart any longer. Even his voice sounded different; it was harder, sharper.

'Well, he got the necessary planning permission, but I want to alter it slightly. Instead of exclusive weekend flats for 'yuppies', I would rather make them into smaller units for local people, farm workers or villagers. I don't think we'll have any problem with the change of use.'

Robina nodded approvingly. Once she concentrated on the work aspect, she felt on safer ground. 'That sounds like a much better idea; although, I suspect, not quite so financially rewarding. That Hay Lane site is in a prime position. It's nicely secluded, and yet has delightful views across the valley. Marcus thought they'd sell for quite a substantial sum.'

'That's as may be, but accommodation to let is almost impossible to find around here. Many of the estate workers have to travel quite some distance daily, and some live as far away as Benwell. I believe it makes financial sense to provide reasonable accommodation for the work force, and that is what I propose to do.'

'So you want to turn it into apartments to rent out?'

'Yes. That is where you come in.'

'Me? Why me?' she asked, frowning at him in bewilderment. 'We've already tendered for the steelwork content. If the alterations are only minor, we will almost certainly stick by our original quotation.'

Brett sat back in his chair and rubbed his hands together. 'I would like you to produce an alternative design — one that should satisfy the town hall planning authority. Base it on the original — use that as a prototype, but make the rooms smaller and more compact.'

'That's not the sort of work I do,' Robbie said abruptly, preparing to get up and leave. 'I do detailing work — steelwork detailing, beams, columns, etcetera — not house plans. You need an architect. I'm sorry to have wasted your time. I don't know where you got the idea from that was what I did, but you were misinformed.'

'Maybe it's not what you do normally, but it is something you *could* do, isn't it, as an extension to the detailing work needed? Someone will have to do it, and I'm sure you could make a better job of it on your computer than I could on scraps of paper. Simon Parker needs some assistance since he's extremely busy, and I immediately thought of you. It would pay much better than your usual work. You'll get the going rate as a commission fee for that part of the job.'

The figure he mentioned startled her. Mentally, she calculated just how it could help out with the family finances with that sort of money coming in on a regular basis. The firm's bank balance wasn't too healthy right now, as she knew only too well, and recently the family hadn't taken much out in the way of wages — just sufficient to keep the home running. Maybe it was another option that she could pursue. At least Brett was offering her a chance to have a go. If she made a mess of it, then it would be his hard lines.

'I suppose I could do it, but I don't see why I should. It has nothing whatsoever to do with structural steelwork or Davison Fabrications,' she prevaricated. She felt like a donkey being fed the proverbial carrot.

'Ah, but it has,' he retorted. 'Davison Fabrications were to provide the new steel supporting beams and hand railing, balustrades, etcetera — even a fire escape, I believe. All of which will still be needed, and your firm could supply, if you'll agree to redesign the units for me. Otherwise . . . ' He spread out his hands expressively. 'Otherwise I'll have no option but to go elsewhere and start all over again with new suppliers and so on, which would be a great shame. Apart from the obvious delay involved, as I said on the phone, I prefer to deal locally if I can.'

'In that case . . . ' She still felt she was being unfairly manipulated. Had Brett heard how short of work they were? Was it a guilty conscience, even? Could she contemplate being involved so closely with him, even if it was purely business?

'This is just another field of work to what you do usually, isn't it? Who knows, you might find it quite a lucrative way to branch out sometime — further your career.' Brett sat forward, propping his chin on one hand, watching her intently, realising her difficulty. He could sense her inner torment, not wanting to turn down any work for the firm, and yet still angry enough with him not to want the project. It was a hard decision to make.

'Come on down to the barn and see first-hand what I envisage, get a feel for the project — or are you too busy at the moment?' he said, getting to his feet. 'My site engineer is down there now. It's a good opportunity.'

'OK, show me what you want me to do.' Robbie sighed. She knew that there was no way she could turn it down when it meant more work for the men. He had her over a barrel. She would just have to keep a stiff upper lip and hope that she didn't come into contact with Brett too often.

They spent the next hour examining the barn with a member of the estate staff so that Robina could get the overall picture of what Brett proposed, and then they returned to the Estate Office. In a way, it was similar to a job she'd done a couple of years back when someone wanted an extension to their house, but that was only small by comparison. Brett's scheme was certainly praiseworthy, and if it had been for anybody else she would have been delighted to take it on.

Robina pored over the drawings

already done, asking pertinent questions and throwing out suggestions in a professional manner, deeply absorbed with the work in hand. It was the only way she could cope. She had to forget the past and pretend he was just another client. One thing was certain: she knew now that she had to find a way of leaving Little Prestbury, but that didn't mean Brighton. Just as soon as this job was done she would have to get away — somewhere, she knew not where.

'You certainly seem to know what you're doing these days,' Brett said, watching her complete preoccupation with the drawings. 'You have earned yourself quite a reputation, I hear. Not many girls would have taken to draughtsmanship like you have.'

'I wanted to stay in the village and help my father, since he has no son to follow on, but I needed something more involved than pounding away on a typewriter. Eric — maybe you remember him — took me under his wing and taught me all he knew, before he had to retire through ill health. Business was slow at the time, so instead of employing anyone else, I took over and did what needed doing. Work seemed like good therapy at the time.' *It still does*, she thought miserably. She glared grimly up at him, and saw the bleak look as her taunt hit home, before she lowered her gaze again to the plans.

'Your father must be exceedingly proud of your achievements,' he said in a subdued tone.

'I don't know if he approves of the modern technology. He is of the old school, you know, more used to drawing boards and slide rules than computers and calculators. I prefer the latter.' As she bundled up the paperwork ready to leave, she asked after his parents. It was a mere formality — just something to say, since they had nothing in common. The Scotts didn't go out much or get involved with the village activities so she hadn't spoken to them since Brett left the village. Though

58

she saw Marcus and Juliet from time to time — usually out riding on the estate and the local bridlepaths — the Scotts kept themselves to themselves. It was a slightly feudal situation, the Scotts at the big house treated like lords of the manor by the locals.

' 'Shattered' is the operative word, I guess,' Brett said, handing her a rubber band to wrap round the bundle. 'It still hasn't sunk in. It was so unexpected. Marcus was the last person one would have thought of having a car accident. If it had been me they would have understood, but not Marcus. He was always so scrupulously careful, particularly when driving in foggy conditions. Juliet's not sure now what to do about the wedding planned for this summer. So much is already arranged, so it will have to go ahead, I guess.'

'They must miss Marcus dreadfully, but at least they have you to look after things now; and Juliet, of course. I heard she was getting married.' Robina watched the changing emotions flit across his face. Unhappiness, guilt, dejection, resignation.

'Why, Brett? Why did you leave me like that?' The question came out quite unintentionally. Perhaps it was mention of Juliet's wedding that sparked it. As soon as she said it, she wished she hadn't. She had been so determined that she would never ask because she felt sure she already knew the answer, and she didn't want to hear it. She couldn't bear to have him spell it out — how naive and foolish she had been at seventeen.

'Personal reasons, Robbie.' He shuffled papers about absentmindedly as if seeking something. 'I . . . I know how dreadful it must have been . . . '

A knock on the door interrupted him and a workman entered. 'Will you do it?' Brett asked, startling her back to the business in hand. He was obviously thrown by the man's inopportune arrival — or was it in fact beneficial from his point of view? she wondered.

'Yes, of course. You must know that

we can ill afford to turn any work down at present. It is still hard to come by, and we have our reputation to keep up. We agreed to do it for Marcus, and a Davison's word is sacrosanct. I'll make a start as soon as possible and let you have my proposals.'

'Good.' He handed her a cheque, which he had already written. His tone was brusque and dismissive. 'If there is anything else you need to know, just ask. You have my number, or you can contact my site engineer.'

'You were pretty sure of yourself, weren't you?' she said snappily, glancing at the figures on the bottom of the cheque. She quickly left the office, her face red with frustrated anger. She wouldn't make the same mistake again. She couldn't care less why Brett had left Little Prestbury four years previously, and she would certainly never ever ask him for an explanation again.

★ ★ ★

'What do you think, Dad?' Robina waved the cheque under his nose. 'That should help the coffers.'

Her father, having just come in from the works, took off his specs and wiped them before closely examining the cheque. 'Good heavens, girl. What have you to do for that amount of money?'

She explained what the new project entailed and what Brett had commissioned her to do, and immediately her father refused to let her deposit it in the firm's bank account.

'No, Robbie, that is a private transaction, nothing to do with Davison Fabrications. You put it in your own account. You've had precious little in the way of wages lately.'

'But, Dad,' she protested, to no avail — he was adamant.

'It looks as if we will still be providing the steelwork, so the firm can send its bill in for that. Go on, go and buy yourself something pretty, you deserve it. We're still managing to keep the wolf from the door, aren't we? Whatever

Brett Scott pays you won't in any way compensate you for what he did to you. I'm only sorry that we got involved with Marcus in this instance.'

If it hadn't been for the fact that the work involved the Prestbury Estate and Brett, Robina would have relished designing the new layouts. The whole scheme appealed to her, and it would be quite challenging, testing her skill more than the work she usually did. Maybe it was something she could take up in the future to supplement their income, she thought. Who knew? Computer work fascinated her, and she was always thinking of new applications for it. Maybe this would lead to a change in career direction.

She'd decided that, since it wasn't strictly the firm's work as such — at least to begin with — she would work on it in her spare time in the evening and at weekends, but her father felt differently.

'I think we ought to get Jim in to do the rest of the Pearson drawings, leaving you free to get on with this Hay Lane one. Jim could do with the work, by all accounts.'

'It will add too much cost to the Pearson job,' protested Robina. 'There'll be no profit margin left. It was going to be touch and go at best. I don't mind working weekends.'

'No, love. If we get a move on with it, I might be able to get a quick payment that will help. We can't have you working all hours, lass, and I hear Jim's having a tough time. He could do with the work. Don't worry, we'll get by. You'll be wanting to get this Prestbury Estate job out of the way as quickly as possible, I've no doubt, and that will be the end of our involvement with that family. Just do the best you can, no-one can ask for more.'

She had to agree; and secretly she was delighted, because she wanted to spend time on Brett's job now: it fascinated her. During the evening meal, she went into more detail about the proposed conversion, and her parents reluctantly had to admit that it sounded like an extremely good idea since accommodation for locals was hard to come by.

'Are you sure you can handle it?' asked her mother anxiously. 'I mean, not that I doubt your ability, Robbie, but how will you take to working with Brett? Won't it be a bit awkward for you?'

'I won't see that much of him, hopefully. I can deal mainly with the site engineer, and it is work we can't afford to turn down. I will just have to treat Brett as I would any other business client,' she said rather vehemently. 'Besides, if I don't do the design work, he'll take the steelwork fabricating elsewhere.'

'That sounds like blackmail. He didn't . . . ?'

'No, Mum, he didn't say anything else; and what's more, I couldn't care less.'

'If you feel at all doubtful or threatened, don't do it, Robbie,' her father said quietly. 'It won't be the end of the world if we don't do that particular job, and anyone with any sense would understand us turning it down. We can manage very well without the Scotts' work in future. I won't have him upsetting you again.'

'It's all right. I can cope, honestly. We don't want to lose our good reputation, do we, Dad? Besides, I told you, Brett means nothing to me now.'

'Well, let me know if anything happens for you to change your mind, Robbie. You're more important than any job.'

'Thanks,' she said quietly. She knew he meant every word.

Robina knew that it was going to be extremely difficult, but she didn't want her parents to see how much Brett still meant to her; or how hard it had been, going to see him that afternoon and spending time on the estate together. If the site engineer hadn't been there, she didn't think she could have coped. She tried to put on a cool exterior, saying that business was business, after all. She knew that they too had been puzzled, to say the least, by Brett's behaviour, but she hadn't felt capable of explaining why she thought he'd gone away. She had been too shattered herself, and as time went by it became immaterial.

She assumed to start with that the measurements on the original plans were accurate, and put the information onto the computer. Then she divided it up, trying to make best use of the space, bearing in mind nominal sizes for each room and the directions in which they faced. She came up with several variations based on the information she'd been given.

By the time she had finished the preliminary work, she had numerous questions she needed to ask Brett — they weren't the sort the site engineer would be able to answer, unfortunately. She did consider putting them in writing and dropping them in the post, but thought better of it. She was going to have to face him occasionally, so the sooner she got used to the idea, the better. After running off some prints showing the different layouts and proposals she wanted to discuss, she rang Brett one Friday morning, hoping he would be free later that day.

'I'm sorry, Robbie, but I'm tied up all day, so if you can't bring yourself to have dinner with me, it will have to be tomorrow morning at the earliest.'

'I already have a date for this evening, so it had better be tomorrow,' she said.

'So, will nine o'clock be too early for you?' He accepted her refusal with equanimity.

'Nine o'clock will be fine.'

Robbie put the phone down and breathed a deep sigh. She had been tensed up in anticipation of an early meeting, but now it was delayed until morning, she had a while before putting herself through the mental torture again.

Richard had asked her out for a meal

that night, and Robina knew instinctively that this was going to be *the* occasion when a decision about their future was to be made. Somehow, she knew it was going to be a parting of the ways. Richard wanted to remain with the firm he had been with since leaving school, so would do as they requested and transfer back to Brighton.

She felt rather sad as she zipped herself into the little black number she had bought on impulse a few months earlier. The dress suited her despite the severity of the colour. She brightened it up with the pearl necklace given her by her parents on her twenty-first birthday, and an ornate bracelet bequeathed her by her aunt Robina — the aunt she'd been named after but had hardly known. She didn't require much make-up normally, but tonight, bearing in mind the likely subdued lighting, she experimented with a touch of eyeshadow and mascara to bring out the blue of her eyes; then, with a smear of lipstick, she was ready.

She took a last look at her hair, which she had swept up in a sophisticated style and sprayed with lacquer to keep the stray ends neat. *Not bad*, she thought with a smile of satisfaction. After tonight she would be back on the shelf, so she might as well make the most of it for now. Slipping her feet into some high-heeled sandals, she heard Richard's car drawing up outside, and hurried downstairs. She didn't want him getting into a conversation with her parents, not tonight.

'Punctual as ever,' he said, solicitously helping her into the passenger seat.

'Hungry as ever!' She grinned, trying to keep the mood light.

'Let's hope the Cross Keys lives up to its reputation, then. A chap at work recommended it, but I've never been there.'

The Cross Keys was a well-known local pub noted for good food and select atmosphere. Robina had been once before in the company of Brett, and wished Richard had chosen some other place to dine. The trouble was, there were so many places with memories of Brett, it was difficult avoiding all of them.

The Cross Keys had an attractive, romantic character. There were several small rooms dotted with intimate alcoves, all resplendent with red plush padded seats. The bar area, with its low ceiling criss-crossed with dark oak beams, had a log fire burning in the hearth — more for show than necessity. Horse brasses and old-fashioned farm implements decorated the thick stone walls. Robina remembered Brett joking about the bed warming pan on the wall, telling her that they still used them at the Grange. She still didn't know whether to believe him or not.

Richard procured drinks while they studied the menu, and then they were ushered through to the dimly lit dining room. It looked cosy, the tables set with gleaming glassware and cutlery, and each with a candle centred in a floral arrangement; soft music played in the background. The lighting was discreet. Richard, immaculately dressed as always in a smart grey suit, kept fingering his tie nervously. Robbie could sense the tension in him, so began explaining about her latest job.

' . . . It is really interesting work, and I might consider doing more of it if all goes well with this project.'

'It certainly sounds like a change of direction from your usual work,' he replied vaguely.

'Oh, it is, and of course I shall have to work closely with the engineer who will be in overall charge of the scheme, but it is quite an exciting career change if it comes off. I might even go to college and do the job properly. There must be courses I could take, even night classes.'

Their first course arrived, and Robina sensed Richard was none too happy with her talking about a career, so she changed the subject. Obviously he wanted a wife who would stay at home and forget about working for a living. Someone who would be happy to devote their time to keeping house, the way his mother did, and listen to Mrs Terrier's ailments with sympathetic understanding.

His steadfast loyalty to his mother annoyed her; but she had known all along what he was like, so how could she argue with him now? He was the opposite of Brett — which, to begin with, she had found comforting — but now she felt she was seeing Richard for the very first time, and suddenly realised how staid her life had become of late. How could she possibly have contemplated tying herself to him for ever? She was young, with her whole life ahead of her. There was a world out there that she could explore. It was time she broke free and stopped recalling all the maudlin memories. Brett was her past, and soon so would Richard be. She smiled fondly at him and tried to let him down lightly.

'Have you made your decision?' she asked.

'I thought we'd decide together. But let's not talk about it for the moment. Let's enjoy the meal.'

As they were nearing the end of their first course, Robina looked up as some more patrons were being shown to their table, and was horrified to see Brett with an attractive — not to say, seductive — young woman on his arm. His escort couldn't have been more than seventeen or eighteen years old at most, but was the sort of person that everyone noticed. Every red-blooded man would, anyway. The men would ogle and the women would tut. She was that sort of woman.

The dining room was too small to avoid seeing each other, so Robina had to acknowledge them. Her heart beat wildly at the sight of him. It should have been her at his side being wined and dined. She should have had the pleasure of sitting opposite him, admiring his handsome face and enjoying his witty repartee. It should be her he drove home, and her he kissed goodnight. It flashed through her mind.

'Good evening, Robina.' Brett stopped by their table. He seemed as surprised to see her as Robina was to see him.

'Brett,' she replied tautly.

For a moment nobody spoke. Brett scowled at Richard, weighing him up like a prizefighter observing his opponent. Robina quickly glanced across at Richard, who had risen politely to his feet, and with a tight smile she introduced the two men to each other.

'This is Fern,' Brett divulged, urging his young lady friend forward. 'She's visiting the Grange for a few days. Over from America for a short holiday.'

Fern eyed Richard, who looked as if he was debating whether he should invite them to join their table. Robina frowned, hoping that he would get the message. She was wishing desperately that Brett would move on, when fortunately the waiter arrived to clear their plates ready for their next course, causing the necessary distraction.

'*Bon appetit*,' Brett murmured as they moved on.

Even though Brett and his companion were seated at the far side of the room, Robina couldn't help watching them. They were in her line of vision without it being too apparent, and she couldn't tear herself away. She could feel the colour rising in her cheeks when Richard held her gaze across their table with a quizzical look. She must have given something away in her manner, she thought. Maybe he could even hear how erratically her heart pulsated with jealousy. Would she ever get over Brett? Why couldn't she accept the futility of it?

The rest of the meal was a nightmare, trying to keep the conversation going, but all the time conscious of her eyes straying to the other table. She felt like scratching the other woman's eyes out and pouring the soup over Brett for his insensitivity. How could he stay, knowing how upset she must be?

Was this girl — this *Fern* — the 'personal reason' he'd told her about? Four years ago, she would still have been at school, surely.

Brett looked ill at ease, and not in the mood for much chit-chat from what she saw. He frowned often and appeared to leave the conversation to his guest. Was he trying to keep his association with the woman concealed? Robina wondered. He should know well enough by now that around here, one couldn't keep anything secret. She wondered what the local gossips would make of it all.

Fern was stunningly beautiful if you liked the classic model type. The tight-fitting dress she wore left absolutely nothing to the imagination, and her figure was one even Richard must notice — especially with the way she flaunted herself! Robina gulped with envy. The evening was turning into a total disaster and it wasn't over yet. She wished she'd pleaded a headache and stayed at home.

Brett and Fern left early, while Richard and Robina were still at the coffee stage. They must have given the sweet trolley a miss, because the girl looked distinctly peeved, and glared at Robina as they passed by their table on the way out.

Robina relaxed with a sigh of relief once they'd gone. She had thought she could cope with meeting Brett socially, but what she hadn't anticipated was seeing him escorting other women around for some reason, or for being so insanely jealous still. It was quiet in the dining room, with few other diners left, and then Richard got round to asking her the question she had been dreading all night.

'I know I'm not exactly a knight in shining armour, but . . . well . . . I'm not very good at this sort of thing, but have you considered my proposal? Will you marry me? I'll hand in my notice and . . . '

She shook her head. 'You really do want to stay with the firm and go back to Brighton, don't you? I'm sorry, but I can't see myself living next door to your mother, and becoming the polite little suburban housewife. I never had any intention to mislead you, but that isn't for me, and I realise now you would be far happier with someone else. It's not your fault. I'm the one to blame. I should have . . . '

He took hold of her hand. 'Let's leave it there, shall we? It's only what I was expecting. I was prepared to . . . but no, you're right. Let's part amicably, shall we?'

Soon afterwards, they left and drove straight back to Little Prestbury, where she said goodnight to him at the garden gate and watched regretfully as he drove away. That was it — all over. She was now back on the shelf — for good.

Robina found herself crying into her pillow, sad that she had to accept the fact she was probably going to end up an old maid because she couldn't marry someone she didn't love. The one person she *did* love obviously didn't love her, at least not enough to want to marry her, and she still had him to face the next morning in the course of the job! She had come to accept that it was Brett she loved — it had always been Brett, and always would be. Crazy, but there it was.

4

Robina woke to the sound of rain beating against the windowpane. It wasn't just a passing shower, but a heavy downpour coming down in sheets. She stretched and groaned. Her head felt muzzy and her mouth as dry as the Sahara desert. She had managed some restless sleep due to the effects of the wine, but it was quite an effort to drag herself out of bed and prepare for the forthcoming meeting. She felt like pulling the covers over her head and staying there for the rest of the day.

It was a struggle even deciding what to wear. Thrusting her legs into a pair of jeans, she found a clean T-shirt, mumbling to herself about who *cared* what she wore — it should be her day off. She had no-one to please but herself. She glared miserably at her reflection in the mirror. She looked dreadful. He hair was a shambles and her face was pale as porridge. *Yuk*, she thought, *what a sight. Time you took yourself in hand, my girl.*

All was quiet as she stumbled downstairs. Her parents were having a lie-in for a change, and Susan never surfaced before ten if she could help it. For once, Robina was grateful to have the kitchen to herself and get her own breakfast. She knew her mother would have noticed and commented on how tired she looked, and remarked again that she was overdue for a holiday. But a holiday was the last thing on her mind right now. If she could get today over without giving way to her feelings, it would be a miracle. She made herself a mug of tea and some toast, liberally smothered with homemade marmalade, by which time she was wide awake and feeling extremely apprehensive, haunted by the scene the previous evening. She felt sorry for Richard, but he would get over it in time, and no doubt his mother would console him.

Brett was a different kettle of fish. She wondered what Brett really thought. Had he been at all upset to see her out with someone else, like she had been? She didn't think so. Now he was in overall charge at the Grange, he would probably be expected to marry someone of equal standing, and there would be plenty of women more than ready to accept such a role. Brett was quite a catch now Marcus was dead.

It felt thundery, she thought, as she manoeuvred her car off the driveway and set off along the main street. The clouds were black and menacing, with not a break to be seen anywhere — hardly typical summer weather. Robina drove the short distance to the Prestbury Grange Estate Office desperately wishing she could have been somewhere else. She wasn't looking forward to the next couple of hours.

The weather was in keeping with her mood, she lamented, as the windscreen wipers methodically swished backwards and forwards. For two pins she would have rung up and cancelled the meeting, but she felt that was being defeatist. She had accepted the contract, and somehow or other she had to fulfil it, no matter what the cost to her personally. She couldn't jeopardise the good reputation her father had built up over the years; or, for that matter, the jobs of all the men he employed who were relying on Davison Fabrications to support their families.

She pulled up on the stroke of nine and, throwing a coat over her head, ran quickly up the steps into the office, only to find Brett hadn't arrived. *Maybe he's having a lie-in after a late night*, she thought dejectedly when she recollected his dinner date. *Maybe he felt he couldn't face me after being caught out with someone else — some hope!*

She spread her paperwork out on the desk, wishing for the umpteenth time she'd never taken the job. It was asking too much of her. Should she tell her father that she couldn't do it after all? She didn't know how she was going to face Brett that morning, and she wondered if he would be able tell she'd spent much of the night crying. Crying because she finally had to admit she had lost him. The sight of his table companion had truly upset her. Although she remembered Brett had asked her out first, so Fern must have been a late engagement, it was small comfort.

Brett arrived shortly afterwards. 'Sorry, I got delayed with a phone call as I was about to leave the house.' He shook his anorak and hung it on the hook behind the door without meeting her eyes. The atmosphere in the room was electric. Neither felt at all comfortable, so tried to distance themselves with cold self-restraint. When Brett's hand accidentally touched hers as she handed him one of the proposals, she flinched as if scalded and quickly put the desk between them.

Robina immediately set out her list of queries, going through them in a businesslike manner, hardly giving him time to sit down. She wanted to get the interview over with as quickly as possible. In future, she decided she would try to make certain others were present at any such meetings — if there had to be any — which might make it more bearable. If necessary, she would ask her father to accompany her: he would understand and be supportive, she knew. He wasn't at all keen on her working for Brett, although he was glad of the business it entailed.

'Because of the sloping nature of the ground, may I suggest we make the lower floor into garages and use the upper floors for the flats? Even if they don't all have cars, those would be useful storage places.'

'Fine by me. It makes sense.'

'Have you a particular preference for one or two bedrooms?'

'A few of both would be useful if you can manage it. I wasn't anticipating large family homes. More starter homes, and for those getting on for retirement, maybe.'

Robina went quickly through her list

of queries, making general notes as she went along. She was trying her best to be coldly efficient, determined to make sure she got all the answers she needed so that she didn't have to bother him again. She was having great difficulty in concentrating, but finally ticked off the last of her questions, and then asked if there was anything he wanted to ask her.

'I don't think so, not at this stage. This is your project; just let me know if there is anything you need some help with or Simon if I'm not around. There'll be someone on site starting early next week. They're clearing the site and preparing the foundations, weather permitting.'

'I had hoped I might be able to check the accuracy of the measurements, but the weather is against doing that today,' Robina said. 'It's not holding me up, but I would like to verify some of the dimensions.'

'You have made excellent progress, Robbie. Shall we fix up another meeting for, say, Tuesday?' he suggested. 'Let's hope the weather improves by then.'

'I can manage to check the measurements by myself. I just needed you to . . .'

'Nine o'clock Tuesday,' he reiterated. 'Down at the site. I have to visit someone down Hay Lane anyway that day, so I'll give you some help. It's not so easy doing it single-handed.'

She bit back an angry retort. He was the client, and one didn't argue with what they wanted, or so her father always said. But Brett wasn't any normal client. She wished now she hadn't mentioned it. She could manage it equally as well on her own.

'Did you enjoy your meal last night?' she asked rather coldly, pulling on her damp coat with distaste. 'I see you managed to find a table companion.' She said it in such a way that left him in no doubt of her feelings.

'It was OK. The Cross Keys is a pleasant eating place. And you? Did you enjoy your meal?'

'Yes, thank you, it was very nice. By the way, you might care to have this back. I didn't know where to send it before, but you may find it will come in handy one day, since I have no further use for it.'

She pulled the small cushioned ring box from her coat pocket, threw it down onto the desk, and then quickly stumbled out to her car. Tears were streaming down her face by the time he caught up with her, she couldn't hold them back any longer, and she had difficulty in finding the door handle. She wished now that she had put the darned ring in the post instead of being so melodramatic, but she had thought she could carry it off without breaking down. She had been so sure she could return it dismissively, with cold detachment, after what she had witnessed the previous evening. She had wanted to show him exactly what she thought of him, and now she had — only it wasn't what she'd had in mind.

He pulled her into his arms, hugging her almost savagely. 'I'm sorry, Rosie, love. Did I upset things last night by our untimely confrontation? I got out as soon as I diplomatically could. If I'd known, I wouldn't have taken Fern there.'

'Why should I care?' she cried, burying her head against his chest while she tried to compose herself.

'Fern is going to be one of Juliet's bridesmaids,' he muttered. 'She was at a loose end and felt like going out. I was delegated to entertain her. The last thing I want to do is cause you any embarrassment. I truly mean that. I really am sorry.'

Robina couldn't bring herself to speak, and merely sobbed as she struggled to regain her self-control. 'Leave me alone,' she wailed miserably. 'You mean nothing to me now. You can have as many girlfriends as you like, I simply don't care. I wish I'd never taken on this rotten job. I wish I'd never met you. Why did you have to come back and spoil things now, just when I was getting my life together?'

Finally pushing him away, she scrambled into the car, desperate to get as far away from him as possible. She was annoyed with herself for letting him see her tears; that was the last thing she wanted. She would have driven off immediately, but for the fact that he held onto the door, and was handing her the paperwork she'd forgotten in her hurry to escape.

'I'm truly sorry, Ro . . . Robbie. Drive carefully.'

He closed the car door while she struggled with her seatbelt, which seemed in more of a tangle than usual, then he stood on the steps: a sad, disillusioned figure, indifferent to the rain saturating his clothes, watching her departure.

Robina gratingly engaged first gear and sent gravel flying as she sped along to the main gates, hardly aware of what she was doing. It was fortunate there was no one else around, since she saw little of the road ahead. Her tears made it difficult to see, and the windscreen was misting up too, but she didn't want to stop to wipe it. Without thinking, when she reached the main entrance, she turned away from the village, and somehow found herself driving along a minor road round the back of the estate.

Finally, she pulled in, and stopped when she realised she might well have an accident if she didn't. Miserably, she stared through the rain-splattered windscreen, and saw she had parked within sight of the very cottage they had been going to live in after they were married. The prospect set her off again and she simply sobbed her heart out, remembering that they had been there the night before he left. That fateful night four years ago! How many times during those years had she come to sit and wonder what life would have been like, if only . . . ?

Eventually, she turned the car around, and headed back to the works and the office. She made herself a drink and sat looking out of the window at the rain, which was easing up. On the horizon, bright flashes of lightening still zigzagged, and there was the occasional roll of thunder still, but it was looking brighter in the west.

The worst of the storm was over. She was turning over in her mind what Brett had said. If she was honest with herself, she knew that she had enjoyed the brief moment when he'd held her in his arms, and would have succumbed if he'd kissed her. The old magic was still there. If she shut her eyes she could remember how it used to be. It all came flooding back as if it were yesterday. The way her head nestled comfortably against his chest when he held her, and she used to listen to his heart thumping, steady as a Swiss watch. The way his mouth turned up to one side when he laughed, and how he used to waggle his ears to amuse her.

But that was all over! What on earth was the matter with her? Only last night, she'd seen him out with another woman, hadn't she? Surely he didn't expect her to swallow his tale about her being Juliet's friend and bridesmaid. This was ludicrous.

'I should never have taken this job,' she muttered. 'I ought to have left home long ago, before he returned. He's nothing but a charlatan.'

She forced her mind back to the job, and started to update her drawings based on what they had agreed, thinking that the sooner she got it all done, the sooner she could leave Little Prestbury. It seemed like an act of desperation on her part, but it was necessary if she was to regain her sanity. She wouldn't let her father down now. She would finish this job even if it killed her. A Davison's word was revered even if a Scott's wasn't.

At lunchtime, she switched off the light and went home with a heavy heart. She didn't feel particularly hungry, but she knew her mother would start worrying if she didn't turn up. She was already aware of the worried glances because she had acquainted her mother with the fact that she had turned Richard's proposal down. Her mother had commiserated with her, accepting her decision, and gently suggested she needed a tonic.

Susan was particularly irritating during the meal with her constant chatter about her latest heartthrob. Robina felt she could scream with frustration. She was finding it difficult enough to maintain her composure without Susan's idiotic observations.

After lunch she decided to go into town, just to get away on her own for a while. Many times, during the last four years especially, Robina wished that she had her own flat where she could be alone with her thoughts. She loved her family dearly, but she never felt she had the privacy she desperately needed sometimes. Most girls of her age would have left home years ago, she knew, but since she worked in the village, it didn't make sense to move out to the town to live and commute in again; that was all back to front. The Hay Lane flats would be a godsend, but not for her — more was the pity.

She wandered round the market-place, not particularly interested in buying anything, but at least she could get out of the drizzle in the shopping mall and browse among the clothes shops to take her mind off her misery. At one stage, she even began to wish she had accepted Richard's proposal. She would have been able to leave the village, have a home of her own, and could at least have made Richard happy.

Pure chance brought about a new outlook on life when she bought a local paper to read while she had a coffee. She was mainly looking at job possibilities, and then she turned to the holiday page. There she spotted it, tucked away in the property-to-let column. It was a two-line advertisement about a cottage not far from Little Prestbury. Maybe that was the answer? If she had her own cottage away from her home village, and yet close enough to work for her father when she was needed, it might work.

She gulped down the rest of her coffee, and quickly went to retrieve her car from the multi-storey car park. There wasn't a moment to lose because she knew the cottage wouldn't be on the market for long. Properties like that were so rarely available to rent. Her mind went over all the pros and cons of actually moving away and setting up on her own, and the more she thought about it the more it appealed. She could take her computer with her and work from home, leaving Jim to deal with the phone calls now he had more or less taken up permanent residence at the works. Maybe they could even take on a part-time typist, leaving her free to explore other computer options like this Hay Lane one.

She drove quickly to the address given, desperately hoping it hadn't already been let. It seemed like a heaven-sent opportunity — surely it must still be available! Something had to go right for her sometime. She'd had more than her fair share of disappointments lately so it was surely time for some success.

The rain had slackened off, so by the time she arrived at Primrose Cottage it was almost fine, with a watery sun bravely trying to appear. The cottage was one of a pair a little outside the village, with a small overgrown garden at the front. There was a sad, neglected look about the whole property. The paint was dull and peeling, and the front porch trelliswork drooped a little under the weight of a rambling rose — Masquerade, she thought, judging from the multicoloured blooms.

Robina pulled up across the road and viewed it through rose-tinted spectacles. With a lick of paint and a bit of weeding, she could have it looking spick and span in no time. It could be a cosy place to live and work. Far enough away from Little Prestbury and Brett, yet close enough to be able to work for Davison Fabrications when necessary. The advertisement said it had two bedrooms — one of which she could use as an office. It looked perfect for her purposes.

Stepping out of the car, she walked briskly across to knock on the door. She had her fingers crossed that her hopes hadn't been raised only to find she was too late. It was an ideal solution to her problems. *Please let it still be available*, she prayed.

The door opened almost immediately, and she found herself smiling when confronted by a man clutching an angry-looking marmalade-coloured cat. 'Just a moment while I unhook this vicious creature,' he said. The cat spat and snarled before leaping down and disappeared round the corner of the cottage. 'There, now; please come in. Have you come about the cottage? I saw you drive up.'

'Yes, I have,' Robina said quickly. 'Is it still free?'

'Not exactly, although I'm only asking a nominal rent.' He grinned.

'Oh,' she said, chuckling at his joke. 'I meant, is it still to let?'

'Well, yes, it is. The paper hasn't been out long. I wasn't expecting anyone quite so soon. Anyway, come along in and see what you think. It isn't exactly the Ritz, as you can see. I've just inherited both cottages, and feel I must get a tenant in before I get unwelcome ones, if you know what I mean.'

'Yes,' Robina nodded knowingly. 'We've had quite a bit of trouble recently with vandals and squatters in the area.'

'Are you local then?' the man asked, leading the way into the front living room.

'I live at home at the moment in Little Prestbury, but I would love to have a place of my own. It's not often there's anywhere to let in the villages. I think it's a charming cottage — or, rather, it could be with a bit of ingenuity. You say you own both of them?'

'Hmm. Yes. I've been thinking of keeping the other one for myself, but since I couldn't be here-full time — at least, not at present — I want someone just to keep an eye on the place. Make it look lived-in, if you know what I mean. At the moment, the only tenant is the cat. He seems pretty wild, and able to fend for himself by all accounts.'

The man showed Robina round, explaining that the cottages had belonged to two elderly relatives — one had recently died, and the other was now in a nursing home. Primrose Cottage had two bedrooms and a tiny bathroom upstairs, and a reasonably-sized sitting room and kitchen downstairs. The furniture was all old and shabby, but serviceable, and Robina could visualise how she might transform it into a comfortable home.

'Now you've seen it, what do you think? Grim, isn't it?' The owner pulled a face. 'By the way, my name's Greg — Greg Holmes.'

101

'Robina Davison,' she said. 'I'd love to rent the cottage if you are agreeable. With a bit of tidying up, it could be quite homely.'

He beamed with delight. 'Well, that's marvellous — and a great load off my mind, I might add.' He looked clearly relieved, his eyes twinkling mischievously. 'I rather thought I would get some crusty old woman for a neighbour who'd want to keep chickens,' he said with a chuckle. 'I didn't envisage any smart young woman wanting to be stuck out here in the back of beyond, so to speak, especially since it is what the estate agent's jargon refers to as 'needs updating'. Why not come next door into my place, and we'll get better acquainted. This is my lucky day and no mistake.'

Robina found herself ensconced in a comfy old armchair in Greg's sitting room, sipping coffee and telling him about her job, and how she envisaged working from home as much as possible. He was a most engaging character, so she found herself telling him far more than she would normally tell a complete stranger.

'You'll be wanting to get rid of that double bed then to make room for your equipment?'

'Yes. I think the larger of the two bedrooms would be best used for my office. Would you mind if I had it taken out?'

'My dear girl, do whatever you want with anything. I felt like getting the rag-and-bone man to clear the lot. This cottage isn't too bad, so I'm making do until I decide whether I'm cut out for country living. You may as well know that, much as I find you an extremely charming young lady, I am married. Unfortunately, at the moment my wife and I are having a few problems.'

Robina smiled at his thoughtfulness. Men were the last thing she was interested in. He was definitely attractive, and in normal circumstances she would have been receptive to his obvious charm, but for the moment she just wanted to be alone.

'I have a flat in London which is where I spend most of my time, but I am quite attracted to trying some rustic life. This seems like a pleasant change from the hurly-burly of the capital.'

Having agreed terms and collected the keys, Robina made her way home, smiling happily to herself now that she had finally made the break. She wasn't one given to acting on impulse usually, but she felt she had made the right decision. This was to be the turning point for her — a whole new way of life.

She rushed into the house, her eyes bright with excitement. 'Mum, Dad, I've got something wonderful to tell you.'

'My, it's good to see you looking so perky. What's brought this about?'

'I've rented a cottage at Little Newby. It's called Primrose Cottage, and it's just outside the village.'

'Goodness, Robbie,' her mother said, looking thoroughly startled. 'When did all this happen?'

'I was having a coffee in town, and

saw the advert in the paper. I went to see it straight away, and it was still available, so I took it. It wouldn't have remained open for long, so I had to make up my mind straight away.'

'Little Newby?' her father quizzed, looking up from his newspaper. 'That will be about six or seven miles away. What's it like, Robbie?'

'It's a little run-down at the moment, but Mr Holmes has just inherited it, and wants someone in before the vandals get at it. He's going to live part-time in the adjoining cottage, and he said he's going to have the outside painted soon to make it more present-able. I thought I could take my computer equipment and set it up in the front bedroom. It will make a super office, and now we are employing Jim more, we could do with the extra space, couldn't we?'

Her father got out his pipe and pro-ceeded to fill it. 'I don't want to push you out, Robbie — you know that, don't you, love? But if you do decide to do more work like that Hay Lane one, then we will need to keep Jim on. He might start looking further afield for a job if we don't keep him busy. I gather he's already put out feelers, and is thinking of putting his house on the market.'

'Yes, I know, Dad. That was my thinking too.' She picked up his drift, realising he could see what she wanted to do. 'I would like to have a go at more design work now that I've had a taste of it, but I would still be able to do the detail drawings if you got overloaded. I won't be far away.'

'Robbie, is this all to do with Brett coming back?' her mother asked.

'Yes, Mum, I guess in a way it is. I feel as if I need some space, and somehow this came up and I felt I had to take it. You don't mind do you?'

'Of course we don't mind, love. We've been delighted to have your company longer than most parents these days, and you're not to worry about the office side of things. Now that Susan is probably going to university I shall have too much time on my hands, so I will be only too pleased to do the books. It's been quite a while since I did any secretarial work, so I may be a bit rusty, but I'm sure the boss won't fire me.' She smiled fondly at her husband. 'It sounds like a grand idea, don't you think?'

Robina hugged her parents. 'Thanks,' she said. 'I'm so glad you understand. I hoped you wouldn't feel I was letting you down.'

'What's he like — the next-door neighbour?' her mother asked, pleased to see her daughter looking animated for a change.

'Rather dishy, actually,' Robina said, grinning ruefully. 'But he's middle-aged and married, although he says he's having a few problems at the moment with his marriage. He's quite a charmer — a blue-eyed, blond-haired charmer. Not the usual sort of landlord. Once I get installed, you'll have to come for tea and I'll introduce you. I think you'll like him.'

* * *

Robina moved into Primrose Cottage the following Friday. With her mother's help, she'd spent two days clearing out rubbish and cleaning it from top to bottom. Now at least it was fresh and tidy, although she intended decorating some of the rooms before long — she wasn't smitten with the dismal wallpaper. It was now usable, the front bedroom housing her computer equipment and office desk. Greg had insisted on having a telephone point installed as soon as he heard about her intention of working from home; he said it was the least he could do. He couldn't believe anyone should live in such an isolated place without a telephone. The men were expected that day to install it.

Robina was so excited, she found it difficult to concentrate on the work she should be doing. Having taken two days off, she needed to buckle down to some serious work on the Hay Lane job; she had no intention of letting the name of Davison Fabrications down. She was more determined than ever to get

Brett's job done as quickly as possible so that she could sever all ties with Prestbury Grange.

Robina beavered away for the whole of the weekend catching up with her work. It was raining outside, so she couldn't go out to attack the jungle of a garden, and she thought she may as well get the office work out of the way before anything else. She was due to meet Brett's consulting engineer on Monday, and wanted to be fully up to date with her side of things.

On Monday, she bundled up her drawings and drove to meet Simon Parker, feeling slightly nervous because of her inexperience in that area. She felt a little out of her depth, but hoped it didn't show. She had come up with what she thought were innovative plans which made best use of the land available, but it would be up to Simon to decide if they were practical or not. He was the expert.

She need not have worried. Simon proved to be a lively young chap, keen on his work and with a wickedly dry sense of humour. He greeted Robina with a wry smile of approval.

'No wonder Brett employed you. You can work for me anytime! There aren't many women doing this type of work.'

Robina realised he obviously didn't know of her past relationship with Brett, and she didn't feel like acquainting him with the details.

'It's the first time I've done anything like this, so I hope you don't mind me picking your brains,' she said anxiously.

'Pick away.' He grinned. 'You might find a gem or two tucked away up there amongst the sawdust.'

Together they went through the drawings in his office, with Simon pointing out possible snags, and ways of achieving what Brett wanted without sacrificing too much of the existing structure. Robina listened intently, eager to learn from a professional. He was obviously good at his job despite his self-deprecating manner.

'These look good,' was Simon's final

110

comment. 'You have an eye for detail and could go far.'

Robina thanked him with a smile as she gathered up the papers.

'And what, pray, does your boyfriend think about your chosen career?' he asked.

Robina was slightly taken aback for a moment, then realised that it was his oblique way of asking if she was free to be asked out. 'Oh, he's quite pleased really. He works in the City, so he's used to career women.'

His face fell. 'You won't see a lot of him, then.'

'No, I'm afraid not. It's difficult when we are both such busy people.'

On the way home, Robina felt pleased at how well she had handled it, and thought that, if Simon told Brett about their meeting and informed him of her nonexistent boyfriend, it would sound all the more convincing. He might think she was referring to Richard, but what did it matter?

5

'It's time for a new image,' Robina said to herself while getting dressed one Saturday morning. *It's time to wash that man right out of my hair, once and for all.* She decided to set her plan into operation immediately before she had the chance to have second thoughts. She drove into Benwell, found a hairdresser, and watched nervously as she snipped and snipped, but in the end left the salon feeling quite jaunty with her newly-cropped hair.

Next, she went on a shopping spree. She bought two summer dresses, both far more revealing than the old ones that she'd had for several years. These were bolder in design, with shorter skirts and low necklines. She felt quite girlish when she tried them on, and realised how much she had let herself go in the past few years. She ought to take a leaf out of Susan's book, maybe, and become more outgoing and frivolous. A couple of sun tops and some shorts were quickly added to her purchases, along with some strappy sandals.

Two days later she called at the post office in Little Prestbury and found her new hairstyle caused a few raised eyebrows, as did the sundress she wore. She almost laughed out loud when a delivery boy nearly fell off his bike through watching her putting shopping in the car. Maybe the tide was turning in her favour at last. She wasn't exactly unattractive; she had a home of her own now, and a job which she enjoyed; what more could she want?

Unfortunately, the sound of a sports car approaching caught her attention, and reminded her of just what she was missing. It could only be Brett's. The exhaust note was quite distinctive. It was too late to hide. Too late to scurry away. She turned to watch, tensing her stomach muscles, waiting for his verdict. She knew he wouldn't go past without stopping.

He cruised the Ferrari up beside her and let down the window. His eyes devoured her, but his facial expression appeared bland and devoid of feeling — as always, these days. She had the impression that he was bottling up his emotions, just like she was. They were like two antagonists, neither prepared to express their true feelings to the other; but maybe one day she would tell him exactly what she thought of him. One day, they would both explode, and it just might clear the air.

Fern sat beside him, dressed in a tight-fitting T-shirt and the briefest of shorts, looking decidedly impatient and unhappy. Robina wondered if she ever smiled. Somehow, she wouldn't have envisaged her as being Brett's choice of girlfriend. She looked much too young, sulky and petulant; but then again, Brett didn't exactly look full of the joys of spring either. He was a completely changed person.

'Not seen you around recently,' he remarked.

'I've been busy,' Robina replied, and continued to sort out her shopping, rather unnecessarily. She had seen approval in his eyes, though, and for an instant she wished they could revert to how they used to be, with light-hearted banter, teasing each other. It seemed such a long time ago since she'd felt young and flighty. She wished she were seventeen again, but knowing what she now knew.

'So I see! I hardly recognised you.'

Robina slammed down the boot lid, the tension inside her building uncontrollably.

'The new style suits you, Robbie,' he said softly, in almost a whisper, then engaged gear, and the car surged forward and roared away.

Robina stared after it until it disappeared from sight, bemused by the impression that Brett always managed to make her feel ... so special, so

. . . cherished. Mentally, she took herself to task, and hurriedly jumped into the driving seat. She didn't need his approval any more, she reminded herself, but she was still pleased by his observation. If Fern hadn't been there, she might even have managed to hold a conversation with him out there in the main street for everyone to see, just to show how mature she was. Instead, she sighed and set off for home, her spirits plummeting again. Why couldn't she get over him?

★   ★   ★

Robina didn't see much of her landlord to begin with. He appeared only for short visits, mainly midweek when she was busy. He spent just the odd day at the cottage, but she kept a lookout for his car so she would know when he was around. Otherwise, the cottage was an extremely peaceful place to work, with just the usual country sounds and very little passing traffic.

To begin with, she found being at the cottage on her own quite disturbing. She enjoyed the freedom to do what she wanted when she wanted, but in bed at night she listened to the unfamiliar noises nervously. Gradually, though, she came to accept the sounds made by the nocturnal creatures outside, and the creaking of the cottage timbers. The sound of the plumbing was somehow reassuring, as was the whistling of the wind in the chimney. Primrose Cottage became her home, her office, and her sanctuary.

The cat made an appearance only occasionally; it seemed quite an independent creature and didn't need feeding, by all accounts. Maybe when the weather got colder, she would see more of it, she thought — she rather hoped so. Occasionally she wondered about the possibility of getting a dog for company. It would make the cottage more homely and lived-in, but for the moment she resisted the temptation until she felt more certain that she would stay.

Each evening and weekend, Robina set aside for tackling the garden — weather permitting. She had always enjoyed gardening, and wanted to resurrect what had at one time obviously been a lovely old-fashioned cottage garden. Hacking away at the weeds, she discovered all her favourite flowers, and found pleasure in the transformation as she cleared each area. The work was hard, but soothing; she could let her thoughts wander at will, and it was unbelievably tranquil.

Gradually, she was getting her strained emotions into some sort of order again. Tucked away in her upstairs office, she worked during the day undisturbed, allowing the rest of the world to pass her by as much as possible. Fortunately, Simon was most helpful and acted as a go-between herself and Brett quite often. She couldn't say that she was happy with the new arrangement, but she was content. Her mother appeared to be enjoying doing the office work, so Robina didn't feel guilty on that score, and Jim was pleased to find work so close to home.

One Sunday afternoon, Robina was on her hands and knees fettling out a border in the back garden when she heard someone knocking at the front door. Feeling decidedly grubby, she was loath to answer it, and hoped whoever it was would eventually go away. It wouldn't be Greg, since he would have seen her in the garden from his own cottage if he'd come for the day; and it wouldn't be her family, for they knew to come round to the back if she didn't answer. She carried on with her work, and it was only as she turned to throw some weeds into the wheelbarrow that she became aware of her visitor — Brett. She flopped back on her heels and stared, somewhat shocked.

'How did you get this address?' she cried. 'What do you want?'

'I had a few queries about the job.'

'This is not exactly office hours,' she

exclaimed. 'You had no right to come here. Why didn't you phone? I could have come to see you tomorrow at the site.'

'I did try to phone. At least, I rang your home and the works several times, but your mother kept telling me you weren't available. It was only when I bumped into your sister that I got your new number and address.'

Robina muttered huffily under her breath exactly what she would like to do to Susan when she next got hold of her.

'I suppose you offered her a lift in your status symbol in order to extract that information from her.'

His lips twitched. 'She did seem impressed to be seen driving through the village in the Ferrari. It made her day when we passed a group of her friends and she could wave to them.'

Robina sighed. 'What was it that was so important?' She threw her gardening gloves on top of the weeds and smoothed back her hair to make it more presentable. She felt hot and sticky, and certainly not dressed for entertaining. She was very conscious of her scruffy shorts and grubby T-shirt. It didn't portray the sort of image she wanted him of all people to see. She had slipped back into her old comfortable way for the day, since she didn't expect any visitors. She hadn't even a shred of make-up on, and was conscious her hair needed washing. It seemed to take more looking after now it was shorter; that was one snag she'd found.

'I didn't say it was important. When I learned you were living out here, I thought I might drop by, that's all. You might say I was passing.'

'Would you like some lemonade?' Robina asked, suddenly realising how thirsty she was — or was it because Brett was there that her throat felt dry and croaky?

'Please; that would be most welcome. It's extremely hot today, isn't it? Summer has come at last.'

He followed her into the kitchen and

sat astride a stool while she washed her hands and got the lemonade she'd made that morning out of the fridge. She could feel his eyes watching her, disturbing her in the cosy domesticity, and wondered if he knew the effect he had on her still. Did her feelings show, despite her rigid determination not to let them? She had kept meetings with him to a minimum since the morning she had returned his engagement ring, and even then she always managed to be in the company of others. This was the first time they had been alone together in quite a while, and she became aware of his disquiet.

He seemed upset about something. She wondered if he'd heard about her fictitious boyfriend and it had bothered him — or had the return of the ring jolted him in some way? Giving him it back had made her feel somehow it was finally over between them. Previously, while she kept it, she could always hope he would return and tell her it was all a mistake and beg to have her back.

'What made you come to live out here?' he asked, looking out at the wild garden she was taming. 'I never thought you would ever leave Little Prestbury.'

'I never thought I would do many things,' she sighed. 'But circumstances change. People change, and I needed space to find myself. This chance came up and I took it. After all, I am not a teenager any more. I thought it about time I altered my whole way of thinking. I have a career to pursue and I needed a place to call my own.'

'So it was because of me! You found you couldn't bear to live in the same village because of me. I was afraid of that.' He gulped down the drink and placed the glass on the draining board.

'I never said that,' she replied coolly. 'Don't flatter yourself. I have a life of my own to lead. I merely wanted some privacy. Living at home was rather restrictive, especially when one has a boyfriend. Maybe you remember how it used to be? The village gossips have had a field day at my expense in the past, so nothing I do now matters one iota, but it's wonderful having such freedom — I should have done it years ago.'

He looked at her thoughtfully and got to his feet. He advanced towards the door, rubbing the back of his neck irritably. 'I'm sorry, Robbie. I shouldn't have come. I shouldn't have disturbed you. I promised to stay out of your way. I had a thought . . . but it doesn't matter. I'd better be off.'

He turned, about to say something else, when Greg appeared at the back door. Seeing Brett, he greeted him pleasantly. Brett looked at Robina, then back to Greg; and, without another word, strode off.

'Boyfriend?' Greg raised an eyebrow inquisitively.

'Ex,' she said, with a smile of welcome — covering up her confusion quite well, she thought. 'Come for your rent?'

'Actually, I came to see if you knew of a good gardener. You are putting me to shame. I haven't time to sort out that tangle out there, even if I knew how. I wouldn't know a weed if it came up and bit me. I don't know how you manage; you're competent at so many things. I think you're quite amazing.'

Robina was pleased to receive his compliments.

'I did see an advert in the village shop window the other day,' she told him. 'Somebody local, by all accounts; said he wanted any DIY. I guess gardening might be covered by the general term around here.'

'Sounds like just the ticket. I'll pop down later and have a look.' He paused for a moment, giving her a thoughtful look. 'Tell me to mind my own business, but I hope I didn't arrive at an inopportune moment, Robbie.'

'No. It's all over between Brett and me. I was annoyed because my beloved sister gave him this address in exchange for a lift in his flashy car.'

Greg pulled a face. 'It may be over as far as you're concerned, but not for him. He's still in love with you, my dear. It stands out a mile.'

'No, you're wrong,' she said vehemently. 'It was Brett who broke it off; and besides, he's found someone else. Some slip of a girl who thinks she's the bee's knees.'

'I'm sorry. I shouldn't have said anything. How about you taking pity on a poor old man and letting me take you out for a bite to eat? I've a few things to do first next door. Shall we say six-thirty? I know a great little place that does wonderful things with steak.'

Robina smiled. 'That's very kind of you, Greg, but there's really no need. I'm perfectly all right. I got over Brett some time ago. He's in my past. It hurt for a while, I must admit. Teenage love affairs can be quite devastating, and I fell heavily at the time. I was far too trusting, but I learned my lesson.'

'If you say so; but I'm hungry, and I would like some attractive female company tonight. Please take pity on me? I hate dining alone.'

She relented. 'How could I resist such a charming offer? You are good for my morale.'

Robina had a lovely long soak in the bath, and, feeling much refreshed, slipped on a silky shift of pale peach. She brushed her newly-washed hair until it shone, and with a minimum of make-up, felt ready for a pleasant evening out. Brett's visit had put a bit of a damper on her mood, but Greg had been most persuasive and she was now looking forward to going out.

She hadn't been out for a meal since the disastrous evening at the Cross Keys with Richard, and Greg was good company. He was extremely intuitive, seeming to know what she was often thinking. It was an easy relationship they shared, with no sexual connotations. It was just the sort of relationship she needed, and it seemed to suit him also. They drove to a restaurant by the river, and since it was such a warm evening they took their drinks outside until their table was ready.

'Do you know,' she remarked casually, 'you have the knack of making me talk about my problems, tell you things that I wouldn't talk to any one else about, and yet I know virtually nothing about you.'

'That's what is so marvellous about Little Newby. I'm treated as an unknown.'

She looked a little puzzled.

He chuckled merrily and flicked a fly away from her shoulder. 'I wondered how long it would be before anyone local recognised me. I had a little bet with myself that I could merge into the rural scene and remain inconspicuous if I so wished. I suppose if I told you my real name was Greg Chandler, you would know me immediately.'

'You mean you are ... Greg Chandler ... the film star!' she gasped. 'Gosh, I should have recognised you. I've seen all your films.'

'You really are priceless.' He squeezed her hand, laughing at her bemusement. 'My dear Robina.'

'I'm sorry . . . I don't know what to say.' She bit her lip; her eyes were like huge saucers as the revelation sank in. 'You don't look a bit like you do on the screen.'

'Don't go all mushy on me. I like you just the way you are — natural and charmingly sweet. I like what you've done to your hair, by the way. It suits you.'

'Do you really think so?' she asked coyly, feeling somewhat in awe of Greg's disclosure.

'Of course, but it makes you look a little more sophisticated, and I rather liked the innocent country-girl appearance you had before.'

'Gosh, I can't believe it. I can't think why I never recognised you. You're married to Melissa Holmes aren't you?' she squeaked.

'Hmm. We've hit a rocky patch at the moment. She's being a little — shall we say — temperamental, because she didn't get the rave notices she expected for the latest production. She's taken herself off to sunnier climes to simmer down.'

'I am sorry. She's so beautiful and talented. And you . . . '

'Enough about me and my problems, I've come down to the country to get away from them. Tell me about you. What went wrong between you and . . . What's his name? Brett?'

Robina winced. 'He's the son of the local landowner, and we were engaged to be married. One day he just upped and left me without any explanation.' She shrugged her shoulders sadly. 'A few weeks ago his elder brother was killed in a road accident, so Brett had to return to take over the running of the estate. That's all there is to it; except that the work I've been doing recently concerns the Prestbury Estate, unfortunately.'

'Is that why you took the cottage — to get away from him?'

Robina looked at him and decided that honesty was the best policy.

'I thought I *had* got over him. After

all, it happened four years ago; but somehow, when I saw him at the funeral, I knew that nothing had changed — for me, at any rate. I know it is silly and futile, but I couldn't bear to see him about the village, and going out with other women, so I felt I had to leave. I'm a classic case of a woman falling for the wrong man, and somehow it isn't easy to accept. Everyone tells you that you'll get over it, given time, but it doesn't seem to have worked that way for me.'

'Well, my dear, you can take it from an old pro like me the young man in question is still deeply in love with you.'

'That doesn't make any sense,' she said, gulping at the raised hopes his words rekindled. If only it were true! Was it possible . . . ? 'He rejected me. Our wedding arrangements were already underway when he jilted me. I remember we were planning where to go for our honeymoon, the night before he left.'

'You ought to find out why he left.

Why he's looking so dejected. He's jealous of me — a man old enough to be your father.'

'You don't look that old. Maybe he recognised you,' she said softly. 'After all, not everyone is as dumb as me.'

Greg smiled benignly. 'I don't think so, my dear, and I don't think of you as 'dumb' — only perhaps a trifle naive. Yes, it is refreshing to see someone like you still exists. Come along, Robbie. Let's go and eat, I'm starving — but you mark my words, that young man was ready to punch me on the nose this afternoon. Heaven knows what the producer would have said if I'd arrived on set sporting a black eye or worse.'

The evening turned out a very pleasurable occasion. Greg was a charming dinner companion, teasing her gently and flattering her unmercifully, delighting in making her blush. After the first glass of wine, she relaxed and enjoyed his witty conversation, managing to relate a few amusing anecdotes of her own. It was after ten when they left the restaurant and tootled back through the country lanes in happy companionship.

'Where are you acting at the moment?' she asked when they were passing through Little Newby.

'I'm just coming to the end of filming one of those period sagas. I play the villain of the piece. I hope you'll go and see it when it's released — probably some time next year. I can do with all the support I can get.'

'I wouldn't miss it for the world. Just wait until my sister hears about you,' Robina said as they pulled up outside the cottages. 'I can't thank you enough for taking me out and giving me such a lovely time. I'll think about what you said.'

'About treating me like one of the local yokels, you mean?' he teased. 'Goodnight, fair maiden, I've enjoyed every minute of our evening too. What a pity I'm not twenty years younger; I'd have given your young man a run for his money.'

'He's not my young man any more,' she said quietly. 'I still think you're wrong about that.'

Robina thought a lot about what Greg had said. She would dearly like to believe Brett was still in love with her, but it didn't make sense. He was the one to call it off. He'd been the one to leave, and he was the one going about with other women. She wished now that she had insisted on an explanation. At least then she would have known for sure.

She began to think up excuses, much as she had soon after he left: some valid reason why he had deserted her without explanation. Had he discovered some medical problem, and that was why he said she was better off without him? That was the only possible explanation she had come up with at the time. Maybe he'd found out he couldn't have children; they had both wanted them. He had talked about seeing his doctor and having a medical examination a day or two before he left.

It was surprising that he was still unattached: thirty years old and still an eligible bachelor. She wondered how he'd evaded all the predatory females who must have pursed him. She wished she knew the answer to her many questions. She wished she knew what Fern meant to him. It didn't look like a happy relationship they had.

She decided that all she could do was to take advantage of any opportunity to make him jealous and see what reaction she got. In the meantime, she had to get on with her life as best she could, and not spend time on wishful thinking. She'd already wasted too long in that direction.

She heard on the grapevine that Juliet was going ahead with her wedding, but on a much reduced scale. Apparently she was getting married in the village church and holding a small reception at the Grange, or so the gossip said. Robina was determined she would be nowhere near the village on that particular day. She couldn't bear to see all that family in wedding finery, especially Brett, who would more than likely be best man. As it turned out, her sister rang her with a solution as to what to do on that day in particular.

'Robbie,' she wailed, 'I'm desperate. You're my only hope. Can you drive me to Cantwell? Tony was going to take me, but he's just rung to say he'll have to work this weekend.'

'OK, Susie. When do you want to set off?'

'I'd rather go early Saturday morning, if that's all right with you.'

'What's the big occasion?'

'Molly and I have tickets for the pop concert. I thought I told you. You remember Molly, her family moved to Cantwell last year? I'm staying overnight with them, and she says she can give me a lift back.'

'I presume you've okayed it with Mum and Dad?'

'Of course. Huh, just wait until I get to university, I'll not have to ask permission every time I want to go anywhere then. It's like living in a prison here. You did the right thing finding a place of your own. You are jolly lucky, you know. I wish I had a place of my own. It's a pity you haven't a spare room and I could be your lodger.'

Robbie put the phone down, smiling at her sister's acerbic comments.

On the Saturday morning, she arrived very early to pick her sister up, and they were well clear of the village before most people were up and about. Robina, deliberately avoiding passing the church, took the long route to the main road, which also had the merit of bypassing the Grange as well. When her sister made no snide remark about the detour, she was most surprised.

'Thought you might appreciate being out of the area today,' Susan said slyly as they left the village behind.

'My word, you mean you actually thought about that all by yourself!'

'Well, no, actually Mum mentioned how difficult it would be for you, today of all days. It was me that suggested asking you to drive me, though.'

'Thanks.'

'You know you could always stay in Cantwell overnight. Molly's mother wouldn't mind an extra one, I'm sure. Maybe we could get another ticket for the concert.'

'No thanks, I've work to do. I may do some shopping on the way home. Pop concerts aren't in my line.'

The journey to Cantwell was quite pleasant. It took about an hour and a half, and Susan kept her engrossed in lively conversation most of the way. At least she took her sister's mind off Brett and her worries while she told of her plans for when she went to university. She made it sound like she was going to a holiday camp, but Robina knew better than to attempt to disillusion her.

Molly's mother pressed her to have another breakfast with them before she set off back. It made a pleasant change, listening to the two youngsters rabbit on nineteen to the dozen, although

Robina realised what a difference four years made. She couldn't work up any enthusiasm for rock stars and pop concerts. The two girls made her feel old and staid with their giggly chatter.

On the way home, Robina made another detour so that she didn't have to go anywhere near Little Prestbury. She didn't, in fact, have any pressing work to return to, so she stopped off en route for a meal and bought some fresh fruit and vegetables in a small market town, after which she wandered round the market stalls for a while, browsing absent-mindedly until it began to rain.

Not very nice weather for a wedding, she thought, drumming her fingers on the steering wheel, sitting in a queue of traffic waiting to leave the car park. She hoped it hadn't spoiled Juliet's day for her. Juliet had always been civil towards her whenever they met, and Robina thought they could possibly have become friends if she had married Brett.

On the last lap of her journey, she

was negotiating a bend in a narrow country lane when the car suddenly veered off left, ending up half-into the entrance of a field. It all happened so quickly that she hadn't time to panic, but felt quite shaken by the experience once the car came to rest. She sat for a few minutes to recover, thanking her lucky stars she hadn't been going at great speed. It was the first time she'd had an accident of any kind in all her years of driving.

Pulling on her coat, she got out to have a look at what had caused it, fearing some mechanical breakdown, but it turned out to be simply a puncture. Sighing miserably at the prospect of having to change the wheel in pouring rain, she wished she hadn't delayed so long over lunch. If only she had stuck to the main roads, too, where she might have got some assistance.

She opened the boot and took out the spare wheel and the jack, and that was when she came up against a stumbling block. The wheel nuts were on so tight that she couldn't undo them. Cursing, she struggled valiantly, but they wouldn't budge. By now she was both wet and dirty, and thoroughly fed up. She'd known from the outset that it was going to be a grim day, and it was now getting worse by the minute.

She was about to give up and start walking to find the nearest telephone when a large black saloon passed and stopped. She watched with relief the driver tucking the car in as far as possible off the road before getting out. Relief turned to dismay, however, when she realised it was the Scotts' Daimler, with none other than Brett driving. She stood disconsolately in the road as he approached, trying her best to appear nonchalant.

'Trouble, Robbie?' he asked with a lift of an eyebrow.

'Got a puncture and I can't shift the wheel nuts,' she snapped, ready to burst out crying with frustration. Brett, still in his morning suit, looked incredibly handsome and desirable; meanwhile, she felt like a tramp, with her clothes streaked with dirt — and goodness knew what her hair and face were like! This *had* to happen today of all days, she thought angrily.

'Lucky I took this road, then. I was trying to avoid the worst of the traffic. There's been an accident on the main road and there's quite a tailback.'

'Don't get yourself messed up, Brett,' Robina said grimly, bending down to heave at the spanner for all she was worth. 'I was about to go to phone for help. The mechanic who put these on must have been pumping iron.'

'Come on, let me see to it. I'm only chauffeuring a couple of guests back home now the shindig's over.'

Robina could see two elderly ladies in fancy hats sitting in the back seat, staring at her inquisitively. 'I wouldn't want to put you out,' she said quietly. 'They don't look too pleased at being kept waiting, and you'll get your suit dirty. I'll . . . '

'Well, they'll jolly well have to wait.

You don't think I'd leave you to struggle, do you?' He returned to his car and pulled out an old anorak from the boot.

She wanted to say that he had four years ago, but couldn't. What would be the use? Any mention of what had happened between them previously, and she would probably say things she would later regret.

'You could always stop at the next garage and get them to send someone.'

'Either you let me fix your car, or you come back with me,' Brett said crisply, taking the spanner from her. 'I can drop off the two old biddies and . . . '

'If you could loosen the nuts, I can manage the rest. I'm not totally helpless. I have changed a wheel before.'

Robbie couldn't bear to look at him. It reminded her of another occasion when he'd helped her after she'd broken down one time long ago. She couldn't possibly go with him, she knew that, so she stepped back to let him undo the wheel nuts. Even he had a struggle getting them undone, but finally he managed it — and, despite her protests, changed the wheel and put the other one in the boot for her.

'Thank you very much,' she said, handing him a duster to wipe his dirty hands on. 'I hope I haven't got you into too much trouble.'

'It's been one of those days,' he remarked languidly.

She knew just how he felt!

6

'How about taking me to this village fete they're advertising?' Greg asked Robina, showing her a leaflet he'd had pushed through his letterbox. 'I've never been to one, would you believe!'

'You'll probably think it's decidedly dull after the sort of life you must lead,' she said with a laugh.

'I came down here to absorb the atmosphere — to get into a bit of rural living. This fete seems to be part of village life.'

'Oh, it is. I'm only warning you not to expect too much, that's all. Besides, what would my boyfriend think?' she said coquettishly.

'Which one?'

Robina grinned. 'Either?' He knew about Richard, and had already grasped how she felt about Brett.

She decided to wear a rather swish

trouser suit Susan had urged her to splash out on. Robbie suspected she had an ulterior motive — hoping to borrow it sometime, probably. When she got it home Robina had been extremely doubtful about keeping it; it definitely wasn't her usual style, and she had very nearly returned it to the shop. She was glad now that she hadn't. Greg would be used to his escorts being what to her was 'outlandishly dressed', so the trouser suit fitted the bill, she thought. It was bright fuchsia pink and trimmed with fancy gold buttons. She teamed it with a frilly silk blouse her sister had also persuaded her to buy, and a pair of open-toed gold sandals.

'Wow,' said Greg when he saw her, and gave a low wolf-whistle of approval. 'Where is the chaste village maiden now?'

'Oh dear. Do you think it's too . . . ?'

'Not at all, my dear. You look ravishing. You'll be the centre of attention today, and no mistake.'

Robina smiled sadly. 'I wanted to

show Brett that I'm not the simple teenager he knew. It will be exactly four years tomorrow since . . . I've no idea where he's been during those years, but it must certainly have been somewhere more sophisticated than Little Prestbury. It wouldn't have been difficult, now, would it?'

'That's my girl,' laughed Greg encouragingly. 'Let's go show 'em. You'll knock the socks off any competition.'

The fete was being held in the next village, and it was there, as luck would have it, that somebody recognised Greg for the first time since he'd come to live in the area. Robina and Greg had visited most of the stalls, and were contemplating buying ice creams before visiting the fortune-teller when a young girl approached them. She had a look of sublime adulation on her face.

'It is, isn't it?' she queried. 'You're Greg Chandler, aren't you?'

Greg tried to discourage her, but others turned round to stare. Soon it became obvious he had been positively recognised, and autographs were immediately requested. He became lost in the crowd, almost instantly surrounded by a multitude of adoring fans. It was some little while before he managed to diplomatically make his escape.

'So much for anonymity,' he laughed, taking hold of Robina's hand. 'This is all your fault for looking so eye-catching. We'd best go elsewhere for those ices.'

The local paper was full of pictures of the fete and had a splendid write-up about the celebrity living in their midst. Robina showed it to Greg when he appeared later in the week.

'Another for the scrapbook?'

'I like the one of you there. You look like a right little number in that pink ensemble.'

Robina blushed. 'My mother thought it looked nothing like me. I think she disapproved. I wonder what Brett thought, if he saw it?'

'Probably wishing he could turn the clock back.'

'I doubt it. I'm just not sophisticated enough for him. After all, he's now in charge of running the Prestbury Estate. It's quite a heavy responsibility. I'm not in his league. I never fitted in there. I'm just a simple working girl.'

'Don't run yourself down, young lady. It's no mean achievement what you have done. You're bright, intelligent, and beautiful too. He must want his head examining for letting you escape the way he did. What more could he want, I ask you?'

What indeed? she mused. The villagers could probably answer that in their own inimitable fashion.

Greg returned almost every weekend after that. The weather was glorious, and together they explored the local highways and byways in happy companionship. Greg insisted she was helping him during Melissa's prolonged absence, and Robina found a mutual comfort in Greg's informal manner. Once the local community realised they had such a well-known celebrity in their midst, the invitations rolled in. Greg accepted some of the requests, and always took Robina along with him.

'I need you there to get me out of awkward situations,' he said disarmingly. 'If you see me looking frantic I expect you to remind me of an urgent appointment, like a good secretary should. I can't afford to upset my fans — it's all good publicity — but it can get a bit wearing after a time.'

'You realise, of course, that everyone is going to talk about us if we keep going about together,' Robina said quietly. 'Won't it cause you more problems?'

'Not at all. Publicity is what all actors crave. I thought you knew. It is our lifeblood, and Melissa knows not to believe all the media reports. If it helps your cause to make Brett jealous, then it will be worthwhile on your part, surely.'

'Well, if you're sure your wife won't object . . .'

The outings proved to be great fun.

Robina enjoyed herself, except for the occasions when they met Brett on their jaunts. They rarely met him face to face — more through Greg's good management than luck, Robina thought. Greg was particularly adept at talking his way out of tricky moments, and certainly didn't need her interference as he'd suggested. He charmed everyone with his repartee and wit.

Brett, on the other hand, looked out of place and unhappy, making Robina wonder why he attended any of the functions at all, except to make her life unbearable. He often had his mother with him, as if he was trying to get her involved in community affairs, possibly as a means of taking her mind off their loss. Greg played his part by draping his arm around her shoulder or Robina's waist whenever Brett was in sight, making it appear they were a twosome. She felt rather self-conscious about it, but accepted that it was in a worthy cause.

The work on the Hay Lane site was

progressing well, according to her father, and thankfully Robina's part was nearly completed. Soon there would be no reason for her and Brett to meet even on a business level. She still hoped to find more work of a similar nature, but in the meantime decided to branch out into doing more word processing. It was Greg who pointed out the potential when he asked her if she could type up a manuscript for him. He'd been working on a play for what seemed like years, he said, and had decided to complete it now he had some time to spare. He was currently 'resting' between parts, so could spend the time down at the cottage and finish the script.

Robina immediately offered to type it, as a way of thanking him for his friendship and understanding. He had been so good to her, trying to take her mind off Brett. It was while she was doing the typing that she realised it was another opening she could explore. She was used to doing word processing, spreadsheets and general office accounts, and maybe other small firms could use such services. She placed an advertisement in the local paper straight away, but it produced little response. She received one or two telephone calls asking about her rates, but they came to nothing. It takes time, she told herself, trying not to be discouraged. Living at the cottage wasn't too costly, and she still had some money in the bank, so it wasn't desperately urgent that she find work.

One day, she was sitting having coffee with Greg — it had become a routine break for the two of them to get together for morning coffee. This particular morning they had taken it out into the garden, and were seated on the lawn discussing Greg's latest scribbles when Brett arrived.

Robina had a dull headache, and was feeling rather low. She had come to the conclusion that Brett couldn't care less about her any more, and had resigned herself to the inevitable, so she was startled by his visit coming so much out of the blue.

'Hello,' she said sombrely. 'I hope there's not a problem at the site?' She rather thought Jim was doing the remaining detailing work. It was only miscellaneous railings and an odd beam or two.

Brett looked from her to Greg, rather grim-faced. 'No problem. I just wanted a word, if you can spare a minute.'

Greg, sizing up the situation, said, 'I'd best be off. Thanks for the coffee and suggestions. I think you're right as usual, Robbie. I'll go and make the changes while they are still fresh in my mind. The old grey cells aren't very bright this morning.' He winked at Robina, gave Brett a nod, and climbed over the fence. 'One of these days I'll have a gate fixed here,' he joked, unhooking himself from a rosebush. 'I'm getting too old for such feats.'

Robina sighed and rose to her feet. 'I hope you didn't get into hot water for stopping to change that wheel for me that day.'

'I only did what any like-minded individual would have done in the circumstances. It's a pity you hadn't got your boyfriend with you, although I doubt he's ever changed a wheel in his life.'

Robina grimaced. 'Would you like some coffee? There's still some in the pot.' She wasn't sure how to cope with the situation. She didn't like being rude, but didn't exactly relish being alone with him. He confused her — upset her metabolism.

Brett relaxed sufficiently to say 'Thank you,' and followed her into the kitchen.

'What brings you to Primrose Cottage?' she asked, still anxious in case there was a problem with the job. It was the only reason she could think of that could warrant him being there. She hadn't heard anything untoward from Simon or from the men in the works. It was always possible Jim had covered for her if there had been an error somewhere.

'No, it's nothing to do with Hay Lane. I . . . I have something I would like you to do for me, Robbie.'

'I'm sorry, I'm busy,' she said untruthfully, raking her hair back off her face.

'So I noticed.'

'That was my coffee break,' she snapped. 'Ten minutes away from the computer screen now and then — it's necessary, you know.'

'Sorry,' he said apologetically. 'It's just, seeing you and him together . . . ' He stood by the door with his hands in his pockets, looking round rather sheepishly.

Robina poured the coffee, wondering what he really wanted.

'Want it in here?' she asked, motioning him into the sitting room. She didn't think he would want to go out into the garden that was overlooked from next door. Quickly, she collected the books and magazines off the settee for him to sit down. Then she sat on a pouffe near the fireplace, waiting for him to say what he'd come about. By now he had aroused her curiosity.

He stirred and stirred the coffee in a distracted fashion, and she watched with growing impatience. Something was bothering him, and if it wasn't to do with the site, then what could it be?

'You were saying?' she said.

'I wondered, Robbie, if perhaps you'd let me take you out to celebrate your birthday?' he blurted out eventually. 'That is, if you aren't otherwise engaged.'

She was stunned; it was the last thing she'd been expecting. 'My birthday?' she stammered. 'That's very thoughtful of you to remember.'

He had taken her so much unawares that she found herself accepting without stopping to think of the consequences. Was he jealous seeing her going about with Greg after all? she wondered. He certainly didn't like him — that much was obvious! Whenever they met, he looked as if he'd like to pick a fight.

'I didn't think you'd remember my birthday after all this time,' she said softly. 'Why the sudden invitation?'

He studied his shoes and frowned. 'I owe you an explanation. I want to explain everything. I know you said you weren't interested, but I want you to hear it all the same.'

So that was it! He wanted to get it off his chest. Her heart started thumping violently. She felt certain he could hear it from where he sat. She could. The pounding in her ears was quite audible.

'There's no need to go to any trouble,' she said quietly with her head bowed. 'After all I can guess why you left, you don't have to spell it out.' She clenched her clammy hands together round her knees to stop them from shaking. 'Although — I suppose, if you insist, I wouldn't mind hearing your version. It's too late as far as I'm concerned, though — four years too late.' She shuddered as if a ghost had walked all over her. She eventually raised her eyes to stare at him. 'I was just an adolescent, starry-eyed fool in those days. I let you down, didn't I? I guess I failed the test. I didn't measure up to the high standards the Scotts expect, did I? Who actually put the boot in? Was it your parents, or was it Marcus? Or did you come to the conclusion all by yourself?'

He appeared puzzled for a moment. Then his head jerked up. 'Robbie, you don't . . . you can't think . . . Oh, no! Good Lord, look, we have to talk. I never realised . . . Let me take you out somewhere quiet tomorrow — please.' He was really begging her now. He sounded horrified by something she'd said.

'Oh, all right,' she sighed, massaging her temples. She really wanted him to go. Her head was now pounding with nervous tension. She just wanted to go and lie down; the headache was making her feel sickly. If she didn't lie down soon, she would pass out.

'Robbie, it was nothing of your

doing, I promise you. I let you down, not the other way round. Look, now isn't the time to go into this. I'll see you tomorrow, OK?'

She hadn't been looking forward to celebrating her birthday alone. It would be the first anniversary of any significance since she had been at the cottage, but the only person she could think of inviting was Greg. She didn't feel too comfortable about doing so, though. He was a married man, after all; it would feel too intimate somehow. She knew she could have gone home if she wanted company, her parents would have been only too pleased, but that hadn't appealed. It was Brett's obvious bewilderment that made her accept his invitation. He looked stunned by what she'd said for some reason.

'Did you say something about some work you wanted me to do?' she asked, the pain now so intense that she could hardly think.

'That can wait,' Brett said, getting to his feet. He stood over her, his face full

160

of concern. 'We'll discuss it over dinner if you like? You look dreadful. Are you all right? Can I get you anything? I didn't mean to upset you like this.'

'I'm fine,' she replied, hoping he hadn't noticed the wobble in her voice. Her nerves were stretched to their limit. 'I've got a bad headache, that's all. I need to lie down for a while.'

'I'd best be going, then. I'm sorry, Robbie. Truly, I never thought . . . I'll see you tomorrow. Seven o'clock, OK?'

Once he'd gone, she flopped down on the settee and closed her eyes, but she could still see his face. A ravaged, distraught face. He'd looked so ill at ease, and she wondered why. What could have happened to make such a change in a man? He was getting more like Marcus every day — so cold, sad and untouchable — a man with no heart. Efficient, but forbiddingly stern. She wouldn't have believed Brett could ever look so defeated.

Eventually, once the headache receded to a bearable level, she crawled upstairs

161

to the office and sat staring at the work she had to do. There wasn't a lot to it, fortunately, because she was now far too uptight to work satisfactorily. Her feelings were all haywire — they always were whenever Brett was near. At times she was almost psychic where he was concerned, and his tenseness had transferred itself to her. What had caused the pain he carried around like a shroud? It couldn't have been all her fault that he left Little Prestbury. He had admitted as much. She sighed and settled to work, trying to put the forthcoming dinner engagement out of her mind, wondering why on earth she had accepted. It had been a stupid thing to do.

Greg popped his head round the kitchen door while she was preparing a salad for lunch. She welcomed him with a rueful smile.

'Jealous?' he quizzed, handing her a pink carnation from his garden.

'I'm not sure,' she replied and thanked him for his offering. She placed it in a vase on the kitchen windowsill along with some others she had collected earlier. 'But for your information he's asked me out for dinner to celebrate my birthday, and he wants to discuss a business proposition.'

'And you know what business he has in mind,' Greg quipped. 'I think I'd best make myself scarce for a couple of days. I wouldn't want to muddy the waters if he's finally taken the bait. When is your birthday, by the way?'

'Tomorrow, why?'

'A dozen red roses might fire things up a little more, don't you think?'

'Oh, Greg. You shouldn't. I don't know why I accepted his invitation in the first place. We're through, Brett and I; I told you. I suppose I only agreed because he said he owed me an explanation.'

'So! You're finally going to find out what's eating him alive. Hmm. I must say, I should very much like to know that myself. It has all the hallmarks of a Victorian melodrama. You should write it up, you'd make a fortune.'

'Oh, it's probably something simple, like his parents didn't approve of me or something. I never felt comfortable when I visited the Grange. I know his brother Marcus never liked me.' Robina still couldn't bring herself to admit her guilty, secret thoughts.

'He must have been mad. They all must be, if they can't see your undoubted charm and indisputable talents. I'm off back to London. See you in a few days. Be good, but not too good!' He chuckled and left.

The next evening, Robina got ready with a mixture of emotions, wondering if Brett wanted to come back into her life. If he did, should she let him? She'd almost got used to her new way of life, and almost accepted she was doomed to be a spinster until she was old and grey. Almost, but not quite, as the nagging doubt kept resurfacing: would Brett ever change his mind? She knew she hadn't got over him, it was just that Greg had been so persuasive and entertaining throughout the summer. If he hadn't been around, she would have spent a lot more time brooding and feeling utterly miserable.

She heard the growl of the Ferrari as it approached down the lane and turned around before pulling up outside. Gulping anxiously, she made a last tug with the hairbrush, twirled for a final look in the mirror, then went down to let Brett in. She'd changed her outfit several times before settling for the demure powder-blue dress. She hoped it would be appropriate. It certainly wasn't suggestive in any way, with its high neck and long sleeves, but it fitted well and she felt comfortable in it, although not exactly sexy.

She'd felt excited yet anxious all day, and hadn't got any worthwhile work done. In the bath she had let her thoughts wander along somewhat hopeful lines, before mentally castigating herself for being stupid for reading too much into the forthcoming date. It was only a meal to celebrate a birthday

— her twenty-second. No big deal, and yet she was pleased he remembered it. She wondered if that in itself signified anything. In the past, she remembered Brett expressing his liking for her in blue, so maybe that was why she'd finally plumped for her final choice, and not the pink trouser suit. Unthinkingly, she was slipping back into the way she had been when they were going out together. She had always wanted to please him, and usually deferred to his better judgement on what was pleasing and attractive. She thought how naive and innocent she had been in those days.

Her heart stopped momentarily when she opened the door, he looked so impressive. With his face in shadow and his hair now longer, he looked a little like the Brett of old. She felt like throwing her arms round him as she would have done four years previously. In those days, she had wanted to spend every waking moment she could with him, and whenever he had arrived to take her out she had been eagerly waiting.

'I'm about ready,' she stammered, blushing slightly at her thoughts. 'Would you care for a drink before we go?'

'No thanks. I've booked a table for half-past.' He hovered in the doorway as she turned to collect her things. 'You look beautiful as always, Rosie. That colour suits you — but you know it always did.'

Robina bent to pick up her bag. The way he'd called her by the pet name caused a moment of mild panic. This time she didn't rebuke him. Somehow it seemed right. If only they could go back in time, she thought. He'd always made her feel so precious when he called her his sweet Rosie. Ever since then, she couldn't bear anyone else to use it. Her eyes prickled. She smiled her acknowledgement. 'I'm ready. Shall we go?'

He helped her into the ostentatious, fiery red machine, and fixed the seat belt for her because her fingers seemed to be all thumbs. He seemed tense too, she noticed, and when he accidentally brushed her breast, she almost stopped breathing. She gasped, feeling slightly claustrophobic sitting next to him in the confined space, and waited with bated breath for him to start the engine.

He turned the key and the beast sprang to life, but he let it idle for a moment. Taking her hand in his, he squeezed it gently before depositing a light kiss on the back of it. 'Happy birthday, my love. Relax.' Then, not giving her time to react, he smoothly engaged first gear and they set off down the lane.

She chewed her bottom lip and glanced at him out of the corner of her eye. 'My love', he'd called her. Was it possible? Was it really possible he was still in love with her? It didn't make sense. He looked so prosperous and handsome in his beautifully-tailored suit and crisp white shirt, but his face betrayed how dissatisfied he was with life. Wealth hadn't brought happiness, obviously. She wondered what had happened to Fern. She hadn't seen her around recently, but she was loath to ask after her. She hated to admit even to herself that she was jealous of her.

'I've never been in a Ferrari before. It's quite something,' she said, more to break the oppressive silence than anything else. 'I expect it guzzles petrol, though, and the insurance on it must be astronomical.'

'Your sister seemed impressed,' he replied nonchalantly as they proceeded along the village main street before opening up once they were clear of the speed limit.

'She would! I gather you had quite a chat with her when you bribed her with a ride. You shouldn't believe all she tells you. She likes to exaggerate. She's going to university soon, so maybe she'll grow up a bit, being away from home. Where are we going, by the way?'

'The Falcon OK? It's fairly new, and

has a good reputation, so I'm told.'

'Hmm. I don't remember ever having been there.'

'I thought perhaps neutral territory would be appropriate in the circumstances.'

Robina watched as he nursed the car along the twisty country roads, seeing the well-remembered hands caressing the steering wheel. Surreptitiously, she observed his profile, and saw the signs of strain etched in the lines round his eyes. His face had a pinched look, making him appear older than his years. At that precise moment she felt sorry for him.

'Thank you for the flowers. Yellow roses are my favourite — you obviously remembered.'

'Glad you like them. I remember lots of things about you, Robina. You're not easy to forget.'

' "Once seen, never forgotten', I believe the terminology is.' She laughed lightly, feeling jumpy by his disclosure.

'How's business? I gather from

Simon that you're interested in more design work. He's impressed with what you've done. I see you're also doing word processing.'

He had been checking up on her!

'Oh, I'm making slow progress in various directions. It's early days yet. Rome wasn't built in a day, as they say. I will just have to keep plugging away. Dad's got Jim in the drawing office now, and Mum's doing the books, so I'm free to explore other avenues. I like computer work, but it's difficult getting started.'

'Good.'

'Thank you very much!' she snapped, taken aback by his insensitivity.

'I'm sorry, that isn't the way I meant it. I have a suggestion to make, and that is why I was pleased you aren't busy . . . but let's wait until we have our feet under a table, shall we?'

Silence fell between them until he turned into the car park outside the Falcon Hotel. He drew up close to the entrance.

'Looks fairly quiet,' he observed as he helped her out.

Robina was glad he'd chosen an unfamiliar place; she wasn't likely to meet anyone she knew and so have them put a wrong interpretation on the rendezvous. Rumours spread like wildfire, and she didn't want their names to be linked romantically so she'd then have to repudiate the gossip. This was a one-off as far as she was concerned, simply to clear the air between them; then maybe she could find some peace. She hoped she could, for both their sakes. Whatever business proposition he had in mind was a non-starter.

'Your usual?' Brett asked as they walked into the lounge bar.

She nodded. He seemed to be going out of his way to please, and although she would have preferred a white wine, she didn't like to say so. They found a bench seat by the window and managed to find suitable safe topics of conversation while making their choices from the extensive menu. They discussed the

172

merits of some of the dishes and seemed to slip into their old ways of easy camaraderie. It felt as if the past four years had been wiped away at a stroke. Robina shook her head, trying to make sense of her feelings, but for the life of her she couldn't understand them. Finally, when their order had been taken, she asked him where he'd been during the time he'd been away.

'America. I still have business interests over there.'

'They must be profitable,' she said, staring at the car keys on the table. 'So what are you going to do now? I guess Marcus's death has caused a few unexpected problems. You obviously can't be in two places at once.'

'You shouldn't judge a book by its cover, Robbie,' he said quietly.

'What's that supposed to mean?'

'The car isn't mine; it's hired. I'm trying to be what I'm not, and to make a good impression like I used to, but it isn't easy.'

She stared at him perplexed. 'I don't

understand. You know you've changed out of all recognition. Before, you were always such a show-off, but it came naturally, you didn't have to act the part.' She paused and frowned. 'It . . . it really wasn't me, was it? All this time I thought . . . What happened? Something else occurred that night, didn't it? What was it, Brett?'

'Yes,' he said hoarsely, and took a sip of his drink before continuing. 'Please, Robbie, will you do something for me?'

'I . . . I don't know,' she said cautiously. 'I'm not sure if this is a good idea at all. I thought perhaps we could meet this once, and . . . '

'Please, I know it's asking a lot, but I want you to trust me. All isn't as it seems. I didn't realise how badly you misconstrued my leaving. It wasn't anything to do with us, I promise you.'

'If it wasn't because I . . . then I don't understand.'

'Something cropped up which threw my life into total confusion, but it was none of your doing — honestly.'

She blinked in amazement, stunned by the revelation. All this time, she had believed she was at fault. 'What would you like me to do?' she asked once she recovered. She was intrigued enough to want to know a little more.

'I would like you to come with me to America.'

'But why?' she gasped, having great difficulty in following his line of thinking.

'I know how difficult it has been for you around here, since . . . '

'You're damned right it's been difficult and painful, and now that I've finally managed to come to terms with my life, the last thing I want is for you to ruin it again. I was getting myself back onto an even keel before you turned up again.'

'I don't want to spoil it if I can help it. I'd like to repair some of the damage I caused if you'll let me. I knew you would be upset, but I didn't realise just how badly I did hurt you. It certainly wasn't intentional.'

'You can help me best by staying out of my life,' she replied, her anger mounting.

At that moment, the waiter informed them their table was ready. Red-faced, Robbie strode into the dining room wondering if she was going to manage to eat anything. The nerve of the man!

'Let me explain a little more,' Brett said once they were seated.

'Do,' she snapped, breaking open her bread roll and scattering crumbs. 'I can't wait to hear what you've been doing while I had to put up with the humiliation alone.'

'I can't explain everything just yet — not here. It all depends on you accepting my suggestion. I know it sounds unreasonable, but if you'll only trust me, I believe this is the best way to clear things up. You've been driving yourself too hard recently, and I thought you could do with a break. Please, Robbie, spend a few days at my place, have a holiday.'

'I don't see what good it would do.

You're a fine one to talk, anyway. Look at you. Have you seen yourself in the mirror recently? What happened to the Brett Scott of old that I knew? The happy-go-lucky, devil-may-care Brett Scott? The one who asked me to marry him despite his parents' disapproval?'

'That is due to circumstances beyond my control.' He rubbed his forehead wearily. 'My folks didn't really disapprove of you; they thought you were perhaps a little young, that's all. Look, I believe all can be straightened out soon enough if you'll do as I ask.'

The waiter interrupted with their first course and the wine list.

'Tell me, what sort of business do you have in America?' Robina wanted to get on to a safer topic of conversation. The evening wasn't going as she had hoped. She rather thought she could keep her cool and have a reasonably civilised meal without getting all het up. She took a deep breath to try and calm down.

'It's a market garden on the outskirts

of a small town in Philadelphia.'

'Is it profitable?'

'Moderately so.'

'So what makes you think that I have any desire to see it?'

'I know how you love gardening. Also, it is only there that I can explain properly what caused my sudden departure.'

She shook her head. He still wasn't making sense.

'Please, Robbie. I know it must seem strange, but you will understand, I promise. I didn't realise you thought I'd left because of what happened on our last evening together.'

'What else was I suppose to think?' She glared at him and sighed. 'The past is over and done with, Brett. I don't want to rake over old coals. I've learned my lesson, and I learned it the hard way. I'm getting my life together again now.'

'With the help of Greg Chandler, I suppose?'

'Greg's got nothing to do with it. He

happens to be my landlord. He's also a good friend, and they have been in short supply recently. Being jilted wasn't easy to cope with, you know. Especially in a place like Little Prestbury.'

'I'm truly sorry, Robbie.' He stretched across and took her hand in his. 'I guess I'm plain jealous. Chandler seems to be your constant companion these days — but he is a married man, you know. He's got quite a reputation with the ladies, and I don't want you to get hurt again.'

His touch was almost her undoing. She stifled a pang of regret.

'Please, Robbie. Take a holiday at my expense. Spend a few days at my place. When you've heard my story and I've explained everything, I'll leave it up to you to decide both our fates. There's someone I want you to meet, and a proposition to put to you.'

That puzzled her. 'I thought you were back at the Grange for good?'

'Not necessarily. I won't go into more detail at this precise moment, but suffice it to say that it hinges on what your wishes are. I don't want to make life more awkward for you, but don't make any rash judgements before you know the full facts. I've a few things to sort out on the estate, but we could leave soon, couldn't we? You haven't any commitments, have you?'

She stared at her plate, not knowing how to respond. She couldn't think straight. She knew she should never have accepted the dinner date. She was merely tormenting herself being with him. She never could refuse him anything in the past — and here he was, offering her a holiday, of all things.

'Won't you at least do me this one favour, for old times' sake? I promise not to make any other demands on you, and I'll abide by your decision, whatever it may be. You could say you hold my future in your hands as well as your own.'

'I don't see why I should go. I don't see why I should have to cross the Atlantic, either. I could easily have a holiday in Britain if I thought I needed one.'

'Maybe you could, but we need to clear up a few things between us; and that, I'm afraid, can only be done in America. We can't go on like we are, can we? You look precariously thin, as if a puff of wind would blow you away — and that is my doing, I know. I can see the way you react that you are finding the situation unacceptable, so I am offering you the chance to put this back on course — for both of us. I suppose, if I hadn't had to return, you would have got me out of your system by now, but as it is . . . Anyway, think it over and let me know.'

Somehow, she managed to toy with the food she had selected, and they talked about the Hay Lane contract, now almost complete as far as their firm was concerned. It wasn't in her nature to be vindictive, and Brett did seem to be sincere in his concern for her well-being, so she tried her best to be appreciative. A trip to America was far more appealing than a day out in France. At one time, the Davison family had nearly gone to Florida and Disney World; but that had been years ago, and something had turned up that meant they never went.

'Now, I guess it's time I saw you home,' Brett said when they had run out of things to talk about. 'You were never one for keeping late hours.'

They drove back to Primrose Cottage in almost complete silence. Robina was mulling over all that he'd said. She knew she could do with a holiday — everyone kept telling her so — but since she had no-one to go with, she couldn't be bothered to arrange anything. She wasn't over enamoured of going alone, and her sister with whom she usually went was busy preparing for her first term at university. It would be exciting to travel to America, and if Brett was prepared to foot the bill, why shouldn't she take up his offer? She wondered what sort of house he owned, and whether there would be someone there looking after it for him. Had he a housekeeper? She had no need to stay at his place if she didn't wish to. She could do some sight seeing, and be independent for a change. She knew Susan would have jumped at the offer without a second thought.

'Care for coffee?' she asked as they drew up outside the cottage.

'That would be nice, if you're sure it will be all right?'

'I can please myself these days. I'm a grown woman, fully capable of inviting whoever I want into my home,' she replied, extricating herself from the low-slung passenger seat with as much dignity as she could muster. 'My reputation isn't worth a brass farthing now, anyway.'

'I was thinking of Chandler, that's all.'

'He's away,' she said, unlocking the front door, wondering why she had offered the impromptu invitation. 'Find a seat,' she said, quickly disappearing into the kitchen, conscious that she was acting rather strangely. 'You might like to put on some music.' She wondered what he would make of the roses Greg had sent. She wished now that she had put them in the office out of sight. They clashed with Brett's bouquet of heavenly yellow ones, and the perfume was overpowering in the small room.

As she prepared the coffee, she heard the song he had chosen, and nearly dropped the beakers she was holding. He'd selected the one tape she never played any more. It was kept at the bottom of the heap for sentimental reasons because it brought back so many happy memories — it was their tune. She couldn't bear to part with the tape, but it always made her cry whenever she heard it. This was emotional blackmail. Her eyes filled with tears, and when he put his arms around her she fell limply against him. She hadn't heard him enter the kitchen, and when he gently turned her round she saw the sadness etched in his face. He felt exactly the same way as she did.

He bent to kiss her — a light, tentative kiss, which merely brushed her lips as if testing her reaction. Thumbing away her tears, he slowly trailed his fingers down her cheek, and then he took possession of her lips once more. She found her hands instinctively wound round his neck as he drew her towards him, encircling her with his arms. The kiss was so gentle yet sensuous, warm and sensitively tender. She felt her legs giving way as her senses reeled. She couldn't credit what she was doing. She was actually encouraging him. With a low moan deep in her throat she hung on tightly, returning his kisses as passion erupted between them. It was like old times. Four years were wiped away in an instant. She was back where she belonged in the warm, comforting arms of the man she loved.

'Oh, my own sweet darling Rosie, what have I done to you? Your kisses taste as delightful as ever. Believe me, darling, I never for one moment wanted to hurt you. Fate has played a cruel trick on us. Let me try to put it right. It's not too late, I hope. Give your boyfriend back his roses. Chandler's not the man for you.'

She sobbed and hid her face, scared by what he might read in it. She couldn't go through any more torture.

'I'd best go before I make matters worse,' he murmured hoarsely, clearly shaken by events. 'We have to talk, though, sweetheart. We must, for both our peace of minds.'

Turning swiftly away, he left while she struggled to regain some semblance of composure. She wanted to beg him to stay — to tell her that he loved her, as he obviously did. Their love hadn't diminished. She could feel it as tangible as ever, as strong as ever, but she couldn't find the words. She clung to the edge of the sink, listening to his footsteps disappearing out of the door, wishing with all her heart that he would stay. She heard the roar of the engine as he accelerated the car down the lane.

Mechanically, she turned off the kettle and sank down on to the settee, let the cassette finish playing, then cried unrestrainedly.

7

'Of course you'll go, won't you?' Greg said as soon as he heard. 'Full marks to him for seeing that you do need a holiday, at any rate.'

'I'm all right,' Robina said wearily. 'I wish people would stop telling me what I ought or ought not to do. I'm not a child.'

'Look here. He's offering to pay for you to go to America, not to your execution. Take it and enjoy yourself. America's a fun place. Philadelphia should be lovely at this time of the year.'

'If I wanted a holiday, I would take a holiday. What would be the point of going all that way? Nothing's changed. For all I know, he wants to introduce me to a wife he's got secreted away.'

'Rubbish. Take a look at yourself in the mirror and then tell me nothing's changed. You look positively distraught.'

'I'm just tired. OK, so I still love him — so what? He hasn't explained why he left me like he did. I thought I knew, but . . . I was wrong, apparently. Now he wants me to fly halfway round the world so he can introduce me to some total stranger. No way. I'm not going through all that again. You've no idea what I went through last time. Besides, there's Fern — his girlfriend. What about her?'

'I know, Robbie. It must have been dreadful for you, but . . . but there must be some valid reason for his behaviour. Brett looks to me to be an honourable guy. Why don't you give him a chance to explain in his own fashion? You need to know. Take the holiday and try to make peace with yourself, if not with Brett. You're heading for a nervous breakdown otherwise.'

'Thank you, Doctor Spock. He's had plenty of time to come and apologise — I haven't been anywhere. Good grief, he's had four years! Now he's been forced to face something he'd rather not, and I don't see why I should make it any easier for him. If you don't mind, I've got work to do, and I haven't time to go gadding about the world just at the drop of hat.'

'OK, OK, I'm going. I was just giving you the benefit of my vastly superior experience. I've got twenty more years under my belt than you, don't forget. When love like yours founders, it really is a disaster. When you give your heart, you give it for keeps. You're not shallow or uncaring, so think carefully, my dear. It's a whole lifetime of happiness that's at stake.'

'That's not like you, Greg, to be so sagacious.' She tried to be flippant, but she was biting back tears. The other night, she would have gone to the moon if Brett had asked her, but in the cold light of day things looked different. So very different. She had tried unsuccess- fully to analyse her feelings, but it would appear she had to stay out of Brett's way if she was to have any hope of behaving rationally.

Greg pulled her into his arms and let her sob and sob. 'I just hate to see you ruining your life,' he said gently, 'as well as my shirt! This was clean on this morning.'

She snuffled. 'I'm sorry. I didn't mean to cry on your shoulder. I don't know what came over me.'

'I'm here if you ever need me, you know that, but I think it's Brett's shoulder you should be crying on. He's the one you really want, isn't he, more's the pity. Until you've resolved things between you, you'll be stuck in limbo. Have a showdown if that's what it takes, but clear it up once and for all. You'll feel better, I assure you, even if you decide you're through, finally.'

When Greg left, Robina splashed cold water on her tear-swollen face, reflecting on his words of wisdom. She knew he was right. She should have had it out with Brett soon after he returned, and not let it drag on. Should she go to America with him? What was there to be gained by doing so? Why couldn't Brett explain right here and now? Round and round her thoughts and questions went in a maelstrom of indecision.

Brett had told her his heart was buried in a garden in America, and only she could unearth it — but hers was only seven miles away. For four years, it had been left withering away in a cottage garden after a wonderful summer's evening of passion and romance. Why should she do what he asked again? After all, he was the one at fault.

By early evening, she was still no nearer a decision, and was about to prepare herself a meal when the telephone rang. She nearly didn't answer in case it was Brett. She didn't feel ready to speak to him until she'd finally made up her mind about the holiday. It turned out, however, to be her mother, sounding extremely anxious.

'Robbie, your dad isn't with you, is he?'

'No, Mum. I haven't seen him all day. Why?'

'I'm rather worried. He got called out to the Hay Lane site about a problem, but that seems like hours ago. The rest of the men have gone home, and I wondered if . . . '

'I'll come over. Don't worry, Mum. I'm sure everything's all right. Don't forget, there isn't a phone down at the site, so he couldn't get in touch if he got delayed.'

Robina knew her mother wasn't one to panic normally, so something must have happened to get her to ring. Knowing her mother, if she'd been able to drive, she would have gone to find out for herself. She hurriedly turned off the cooker and ran out to the car. Her father was always so careful. She'd never known him have a serious injury on any of the building sites in over twenty years in business, but there was always a first time for everything, wasn't there?

Twenty minutes, later she drew up

outside the works, and her mother rushed out to meet her, wringing her hands with worry. 'I didn't know what to do. He's still not back, and it's not like your father not to ring when he's been delayed. I didn't know who else to call.'

'It's all right, Mum. I'm sure he's just got held up somewhere. Look, you go home and start preparing tea, and I'll get down to the site and see what's what. I'll ring you as soon as I know anything, or I'll bring him home so you can give him a piece of your mind.'

Her mother gave her a watery smile. 'Thanks, love. You're probably right. I don't know why I panicked; I had this funny feeling . . . Women's intuition, I suppose your dad would call it. I'm probably worrying unnecessarily, but somehow . . . I don't know.'

Robina sped off, more worried than she let on. She too sensed there was a problem. It had been some time since she'd visited the site, and she felt guilty. What if her dad had been having problems, but hadn't said anything? Usually, she would have visited the site more while the men were working, but in this case she had purposely gone after hours just to keep tabs on how it was progressing. She had thought all was going supremely well, and was feeling chuffed to see her plans taking shape. Even when the steelwork part of the contract was finished, she would continue to keep an eye on it. She was looking forward to its completion.

As she approached Hay Lane, all seemed quiet and normal, with little passing traffic. At that time of the day it was rare to see a soul, unless maybe a dog lover exercising their pets. She spotted Brett's car parked just inside the perimeter fencing, but there was no sign of him, or her father's Land Rover. She pulled up at the gates, but found only one man left, and he was closing up for the night. She didn't recognise him, but she wound down the window and called out to him anxiously.

'Have you seen my father — Mr

Davison from Davison Fabrications?'

'Why yes, miss. Haven't you heard? He went to the hospital — oh, about an hour or more ago. There's been some sort of accident.'

Robina gulped. 'What happened? Is it serious?' she croaked.

'Don't think so. I only got here myself as Mr Scott was leaving with the two of them in the Land Rover. They looked like walking wounded at any rate, if that's any consolation. Your father was driving, so I guess he was OK.'

Robina thanked him, turned the car around and roared off, now extremely perturbed. She decided to go straight to the hospital before contacting her mother, so as not to alarm her unnecessarily. At least she had to know how serious it was before ringing. They would have let them know if he was badly hurt, surely? Brett would have telephoned. She wondered why he hadn't done so. He would know they would be concerned. If they hadn't called the ambulance, then they must be reasonably all right, she thought rationally. The first person she saw when she entered the Casualty department was her father.

'Are you all right?' she asked, surprised and relieved to see him in one piece.

'Sure, honey, thanks to Brett.'

Robina was startled: it had been 'Mr Scott' — or worse — for the past few weeks. Neither of her parents had been happy about working for him. Now it was 'Brett', was it? That was a turn-up for the books.

'Mum's worried sick,' she scolded.

'I'm just about to ring her. I tried earlier, but the lines were down.'

'Well, be prepared for an earwigging then,' she said, grinning with relief. 'What on earth happened?'

'Terry, the young apprentice, was having trouble with the last section of balustrading. I was talking to Brett about another problem when the panel broke free and crashed down on the

197

pair of us. Brett's quick reaction saved me — he pushed me out of the way, but the panel clipped him, unfortunately.'

'Are you sure you are all right?'

He nodded. 'It's Brett I'm worried about. I think he might have a broken arm.'

'Oh dear, no. Mum guessed there was a problem, and she's getting herself all steamed up. Why don't you go back and reassure her? I'll see Brett gets home safely. You look as if you could do with a brandy.'

'If you are sure you don't mind, love, it could certainly help. I'm a bit worried about how it might affect us — financially, I mean. He could sue us. It could be a bit tricky.'

'I don't think Brett would do that,' Robina said staunchly, but going all hot under the collar at the very thought. Nothing like this had happened before that she was aware of. They'd had accidents, naturally, but they had been minor ones, and only involved members of their own staff.

'If you could sound him out, casual like . . . '

'I'll do what I can of course, Dad, but I'm sure there's nothing to worry about on that score.'

Robina sat in the waiting room for what seemed like ages, deliberating on how she should best handle the situation. She wondered if the accident had in any way altered things between her and Brett. Would he still want her to take the holiday after what had happened? If he'd broken his arm, it would be a while before he could go anyway, probably. Eventually Brett came down the corridor looking rather ashen, with his coat over his shoulder and his arm in a sling. He didn't look at all pleased.

'Thank you for coming, but I could always have got a taxi,' he said grimly.

'Dad asked me to see you got home safely,' she said, appalled by the sight of him. She had convinced herself that he would appear fully fit and well, and there would be nothing to worry about.

She had never seen him look so uncomfortable — so helpless. 'I had better follow his instructions. It's the least I can do in the circumstances. Are you all right apart from your arm?'

'I'll live,' he replied wanly. 'They've patched me up and given me some painkillers.'

'Come along, then; my car's right outside. I may even have got a parking ticket by now. I'm not sure if it was in a legitimate area. I simply parked as close as I could. I'll drive you home.' She knew she was gabbling, but couldn't stop herself. Somehow he made her nervous. She'd spent the last quarter of an hour thinking how appalled she would be if anything more serious had happened to him. What if he'd been killed! That thought horrified her.

Once their journey was underway, she felt slightly easier, since she had to concentrate on her driving, which helped. Brett sat in a subdued mood, looking a little cramped in the passenger seat. She couldn't think what to say, and Brett seemed preoccupied, so they drove in silence.

'Take the next right,' he said suddenly when they were nearly back at the village.

Quickly looking in the mirror to see the road was clear, she made the turn instinctively, and then realised where they were going. She looked across at Brett, who gave her a sad, rueful smile. A short while later, Robina pulled up, without being asked, on the grass verge, but left the engine idling.

'It was on such an evening as this wasn't it?' he said quietly. Taking hold of her hand, he stroked it gently, soothingly. 'Funny, I can almost smell the scent of the roses even now.' He sighed. 'Oh, to be able to turn the clock back. If only we could have our lives over again, knowing what we know now . . .'

'Who lives here now?' she asked in a strangled voice.

'It's a holiday cottage. Marcus let it out at an exorbitant rent. He was always more financially prudent than me — if a little insensitive, I think. I wanted you to have it. But of course he was right. It needed an awful lot doing to it to make it habitable.'

She nodded sadly, and removed her hand in order to engage first gear.

'The lease is up soon, and I'm not renewing,' Brett remarked as they passed the garden gate.

'Not such a hard-headed business-man as Marcus, I take it. The Grange?' she asked crisply. 'Or do you have anywhere else to go?' She was striving to keep her emotions under control.

'Home, please.'

She turned to look at him. His face had lost its colour. 'Are you sure you're OK?'

'Hmm, positive. The nurse was very thorough,' he said flippantly. 'It's not broken thank goodness.'

Robina drove sedately on to the Grange and dropped him off at the door, relieved when nobody came out to greet them. She couldn't face meeting anyone at that moment, especially not his parents. She wished she knew what was going through Brett's mind. What all the mystery was about.

'Can you manage?' she asked, remaining securely in her seat. He seemed to be having a struggle turning to get out of the passenger seat.

'Feel like coming and tucking me up in bed?' he asked with a spark of the old Brett surfacing.

'I can just imagine what your parents would say! Go on, I've got to go and report to Dad. He was extremely worried about you.' She didn't wait to see him go indoors, but hurtled off down the drive, her face flushed and her nerves in shreds.

In the middle of the next morning, the phone rang. It was Brett.

'I need a chauffeur.'

'I beg your pardon?'

'This injury I sustained was caused by mismanagement on behalf of Davison Fabrications, so I suggest that you can best rectify things by acting as my chauffeur.'

'Oh, but . . . ' Robina sighed, and realised she would have to do as he suggested. Her father couldn't be expected to do it, and there was no one else they could reasonably ask. 'What do you want me to do?'

'I have to go to Benwell this afternoon. I'll be in the estate office at one-thirty. Will you pick me up there?'

'Yes, OK,' she agreed. He hadn't sounded very amenable. She hoped he wasn't going to press for damages now he'd had time to reflect. She could well imagine how irksome an arm in a sling would be, especially to him. If she had to drive him about for the odd day or so as recompense, it would be extremely wearing on the nerves, but cheaper for the firm.

She spent an hour cleaning and polishing her car, trying to make it more presentable. It was only a small runabout, and not exactly brand new, but it suited her and her pocket. It had been the best she could afford, and was her pride and joy. She checked the oil and water levels, and even the tyre pressure, determined it wouldn't let her down. Brett might be used to better things, she thought; but he'd just have to accept what she had to offer, and like it. Beggars couldn't be choosers.

She drove to the estate office in plenty of time, stopping on the way to fill up with petrol. Brett met her outside and got into the passenger seat. 'Good. You're early. I'd rather we picked up the Ferrari before anything happens to it. Think you can manage to drive it all right?'

'Gosh, I don't know. Couldn't you get one of your workers to bring it back?'

'No. I'd rather you drove me to Benwell in it. You can leave your car at the site, and I'll have someone drive it up to the house where you can pick it up later.'

She stared at him in bewilderment.

'This damned arm being out of

action is most aggravating. Have you any idea how irritating it is being limited like this?'

'I'm sorry. I know it must be awkward. I'll do what I can to help in any way possible,' she said, accepting the inevitable. She drove off smoothly, congratulating herself on her gear change. 'I'd feel happier driving my own wheels, though. My car won't let us down, I promise you.'

'Well, I'd much rather you drove the Ferrari. It will be good experience for you.'

She bit her tongue, trying to think of a satisfactory reason for not doing as he asked. From his tone, she gathered that he would brook no argument.

'Don't go booking anything for the next few days, either,' he growled. 'Tell your boyfriend too. I'm not sure what my commitments are yet, so you'd best make yourself freely available.'

Robbie smothered an unprintable oath and gripped the steering wheel. If she was going to have to put up with him in his present mood for any length of time, she was going to have to control her temper. It wouldn't help either of them to have another accident due to her incompetence.

She drove on down to the Hay Lane site without another word. Brett had her park near the entrance, gave the keys to the foreman, and told him to have someone take her car back to the estate office during the afternoon. Robina was next installed in the driving seat of the Ferrari and instructed on the technicalities of driving the superior machine. She could do it if she tried. She wouldn't back out now, and it helped when she imagined how envious Susan would be when she told her. It was one thing to have Brett give her a lift, and quite another to actually drive the car.

She felt extremely apprehensive to begin with, as she manoeuvred it on to the road with all the men on site watching. She stalled it once as she reversed clear of the fence, and had to edge it past the site hut. She could feel her face growing red with nervousness, and was afraid she'd never get the hang of the temperamental clutch.

'Slowly does it,' Brett said. 'You're doing fine.'

She gulped. 'I'll be all right when we're on the open road.'

She was determined to master it. She only wished she'd had it to herself for a while until she'd got the hang of it. She had in the past driven various vehicles, but nothing quite like the Ferrari.

'Right, let's go. I have an appointment at the bank at half-past two, and I don't care to be late.'

By the end of the day, Robina's nerves were shattered. Driving the car was bad enough, but to have Brett sitting there next to her was definitely unnerving. She didn't know how she was going to cope with it day in, day out, and yet there didn't seem to be any alternative. He hadn't said anything about making a claim against them, so she never mentioned it either. She wondered for how long she would have to act as his chauffeur. He hadn't said when his next visit to the hospital was to be, and with the mood he was in, it was not the time to ask.

The next day was little better. Brett had to visit various parts of the estate so they used the Land Rover. At least Robina felt more comfortable driving that, but it also involved her having lunch with him. This they had at a small country pub: sandwiches and drinks, sitting outside in the sunshine. Brett was in a subdued mood, but she learned that Fern had gone back to America, and Juliet was still away somewhere in the Caribbean, which was why Robina had been coerced into acting as chauffeur. The proposed visit to America wasn't mentioned. Brett was concentrating purely on estate matters, and she was loath to bring the subject up.

His injury made him morose and irritable, which she could well understand. When she asked how he was feeling, she nearly got her head bitten off. She quite enjoyed driving, but disliked having a passenger who obviously disapproved of her driving style, even though he never said a word. She tried to remain distant and cool towards him, reminding herself she was a chauffeur doing a job, and that was all — but it wasn't easy.

The next day, they were to go and see Simon at his office. Robina slept badly, and was late getting up, so wasn't in the best of moods when she collected Brett from the estate office. She had been in such a rush that she had burnt the toast while trying to do too many jobs at once. As usual, when one thing went wrong, everything else contrived to make her late. A button flew off her blouse that meant changing into a jumper, and the phone rang as she was halfway out of the door. She did contemplate not answering, but then thought it just might be Brett ringing to cancel. Unfortunately, it was a woman responding to her advertisement, and it took a while for her to discover she was wasting her time.

Brett insisted she drive the Ferrari again, which added to her despondency. It was obviously going to be one of those days when everything went wrong, and she was terrified of damaging the car. If that happened, goodness knew how much it would cost.

Once they were under way, Brett casually asked her if she was going to do more work for Simon in the future.

'No, I'm not,' she said snappily. 'There really was no need for me to do the drawings for the Hay Lane job, was there? You got Simon to employ me as a favour. Right?'

He chewed his lip but said nothing.

'Why, Brett? I didn't think about it at the time, but I'm not qualified for that sort of work. What if I'd made a real hash of it?' She braked hard and tucked back behind a lorry, causing Brett to wince.

'Simon was busy. He was prepared to

turn me down because of his workload. He did the preliminary work, as you know. Since he needed a little assistance, and I thought it was something you could do, I suggested it and he agreed. I had every faith in your capabilities. It was no big deal.'

'Thanks,' she said sarcastically. 'It was only the other morning I realised how I'd been set up. I was seriously thinking I could do more work like that. I didn't realise I was being patronised.'

'That's not how it was. Simon is very impressed with what you did. He would like you to work in his office.'

'I know. He's already asked me, but I'm going to turn him down. That was when it came to me about your manipulative involvement. Anyway, I've decided to go away. I've had enough. I should have gone a long time ago.'

'Where?' he asked quickly. 'Where will you go?'

'Somewhere — anywhere. Far, far away from Little Prestbury; somewhere you'll not find me,' she snapped, her eyes glistening and close to tears. She had no idea where she could run to, but she knew she had to get away — and fast. The last few days had been too nerve-racking by half.

He looked startled and asked her to pull in at the next layby.

'I'm all right — there's no need. I am fulfilling my obligations to the best of my ability. Don't concern yourself . . . '

'Please do as I ask, Robbie,' he snapped.

She found a field entrance, which sufficed, stopped the car with a great sigh, and continued to stare straight ahead, her hands gripping the steering wheel as if her life depended upon it.

'There's no need for you to leave,' he said quietly. 'I'm the one who should go, if that is how you feel. I had hoped you would give me one last chance. I know I don't deserve it in your eyes, but suffice it to say I have your wellbeing at heart as well as my own. I was speaking the truth the other night. I would like an opportunity to put my

213

case. I hoped you might have accepted my offer.' His shoulders drooped despondently.

'It doesn't make any sense . . . ' she murmured, thumping the wheel and turned to look at him, desperately wanting to understand.

He looked into her eyes and saw the raw hurt and sadness. 'I'm sorry. I've been like a bear with a sore head recently, haven't I?' Slowly, he pulled her towards him, wrapping his one good arm around her. She went hypnotically into his embrace.

'I know, my love, I know. I'm so very sorry any of this ever happened.' He kissed her and she reciprocated. As always, she gave way and let her senses take over.

'Will you go to America?' Brett pleaded. 'Please? Give me once last chance.'

In the end, she gave in. It seemed as if she would get no peace until she'd had a holiday. Everyone was badgering her to go somewhere, so it might as well be America as anywhere else.

8

'It's all right for a seasoned traveller like you, Greg.' Robina sighed, unintentionally giving away her apprehension about travelling so far afield. America was somewhere she had only ever dreamed about and never expected to visit. 'I've never been further than Spain before, and usually I've gone with my family.'

'If it makes you any happier, I'll arrange to travel with you. I suppose I should go over to see Melissa and ask if she has any intention of returning in the near future. I think it might work out very well, now she's in New York. How about it?'

Robina smiled warily. She knew Brett wouldn't be too pleased by such an arrangement. 'Everyone seems determined to nursemaid me.'

'Relax and let them, then. I certainly don't mind. It's good for my image,

215

having a beautiful young lady to escort.'

Once the decision had been made, Robina wavered between curiosity about Brett's house and business interests to being anxious and downright apprehensive. Could it possibly be that he wanted her to run the market garden? Was that what he wanted to show her? Who did he want her to meet?

'You are all right, aren't you, Robbie?'

'Yes, I'm fine thanks, Greg. This is fantastic. I've never been on a jumbo jet before.'

'Hmm. Brett didn't look too chuffed when we met up at the airport.'

'He didn't know we were travelling together. I hadn't told him. He's jealous of you. Even when I said you were going to stay with your wife in New York, he didn't believe me. I could tell.'

'Does he think we're having a fling or something?' Greg asked with a furtive grin.

'Yes, I think he does,' Robina

whispered, conscious of the other passengers overhearing. She blushed with embarrassment. Being with a well-known personality had its drawbacks.

'If Melissa stays away much longer, I might just be tempted.' He laughed and squeezed her hand. 'You look delightfully innocent, my child. I wouldn't relish tangling with your boyfriend, though. He'd probably make mincemeat of me.'

'He's not my boyfriend, I keep telling you. I don't know how I was talked into this.'

Robina turned to look out of the window at the clouds. She felt altogether too unworldly, and did so wish she could be more confident and self-assured. She had lived far too long in obscurity, never straying far from the tight little community in which she had been brought up. Was that partly why Brett had left? Was she too childlike and immature? She thought about that woman at the Cross Keys — Fern. She had looked far more self-assured and confident than Robina, even though she was probably at least two or three years younger. Fern would be quite at home sitting beside Greg, teasing and flirting with him. She wouldn't blush like a schoolgirl all the time. Even Susan knew how to cope better than her sister did.

Robina was especially grateful for Greg's company and assistance on the trip, though. He seemed to know instinctively where to go or who to ask. He certainly made the long flight enjoyable. Sleep was definitely not on the cards; she was far too uptight.

When they landed in New York, it was so daunting that Robina knew she would probably have turned straight round and returned home if it hadn't been for Greg. Everywhere was so big and dynamic. The noise and the hurly-burly made feel very insecure, so she stayed close to Greg as he made his way unerringly through the maze of people. He delayed going to meet his wife until he'd made certain she caught the right train. He even paid the taxi fare from the airport, and wouldn't accept her share. She felt she would be forever in his debt.

'Now, don't forget to ring me if you change your mind about staying. I can soon hop down and pick you up. New York is quite a town. I'm sure we could find something to interest you. I don't want you sitting around moping,' Greg said, stowing away her suitcase and handing her some bulky fashion magazines to read on the journey. 'Relax and enjoy the break.'

'I will,' she promised. 'I'll be all right, honestly. Brett will be here before I know it. You go and see Melissa. I hope everything works out all right for you. She's the one that needs you now.'

'I'm not so sure about that,' he growled. 'Take care, young Robbie. See you soon — and chin up, it might never happen.'

Robina settled back to try and regain her confidence now that she was alone.

She kept telling herself it was a holiday and she should be enjoying herself, but she felt so bereft, being by herself in a foreign country, even though the people spoke English. She tried to take an interest in the countryside as it flashed by the window, but her thoughts and fears kept intruding. The other passengers were all very pleasant, and seemed especially interested when they heard she was from England. They helped make the journey more comfortable. In the latter part of the journey, though, she was left alone with her thoughts. Bewildering thoughts.

The last few days had been so hectic. Since she hadn't any work that needed her urgent attention, she had been hustled by everyone into accepting Brett's offer. She knew they were concerned for her wellbeing, and even her parents agreed it was a chance not to be missed. Her sister had been envious, declaring that she would rather go to America than university, before telling her to make the most of the golden opportunity.

When Brett had arrived at the cottage two days before they were to leave and told her something had come up so he couldn't fly out with her, she had been ready to call the whole thing off. It had taken a good deal of persuasion on his part to convince her that perhaps it was for the best. She could spend a few days unwinding first before he arrived. He promised to catch the earliest possible flight he could.

She recalled how annoyed he had been when Greg, arriving back from London, had called in for some fresh milk. It was an arrangement they had, whereby Robina kept a supply of milk in the fridge and Greg was welcome to help himself if he ran out. If she wasn't there, he had keys so he could get in. Greg said afterwards that he had seen the Ferrari parked outside, so hadn't known whether it was prudent to ring the bell or not, but was gasping for some coffee. On this occasion, he had thought it best to creep in to the kitchen by the back door and try not to disturb them. Unfortunately, Brett had heard the fridge door close and had gone to investigate, thinking it was an intruder. He really didn't like Greg, not one little bit.

The problem was, Robina couldn't get over the feelings that resurfaced whenever Brett kissed her, and yet she still felt uncertain about the future. She knew she had to find out what had happened four years ago — it was a mystery she would like resolved. She couldn't see why Brett insisted on revealing everything in America; it didn't make much sense.

By the time the train reached its destination and she had procured a taxi to take her to Brett's bungalow, Robina was exhausted. Everyone had been most helpful, but she'd found the journey both nerve-racking and tiring, so when the driver offloaded her case she paid him, picked it up, and walked wearily to the front door. She felt she could sleep the clock round. She was so tired that she did no more than have a quick look round before choosing one of the beds at random, slipping off her suit, and stumbling under the duvet. She was asleep almost instantly.

A distant bell raucously ringing woke her. For a moment she couldn't focus. The noise went on and on. Prising her eyes open cautiously, she stared at the unfamiliar surroundings, and still the bell kept ringing insistently. Gradually, her befuddled brain started to function, and she realised it was the telephone on the bedside table summoning her attention. She stretched out her hand and grasped the receiver.

'Robbie, Robbie. Are you all right?'

'Yes,' she mumbled incoherently.

'Thank goodness. I've been ringing for ages.'

'You woke me up,' Robina said between yawns, hauling herself into a sitting position. Gradually she reoriented herself and remembered that she was in America. 'What time is it?'

'It should be about nine o'clock your

time,' Brett said, more calmly now. 'I'm sorry if I disturbed you. I just wanted to know you arrived all right.'

'I had a good trip, but found it rather tiring. Heaven knows how long I've slept.'

'It will do you good. Take it easy, and I hope to be with you at the weekend, all being well. I'm looking forward to getting everything cleared up.'

'I wish I knew what you're talking about.'

'You will soon, I promise. I love you, Rosie, just remember that.'

Robina struggled out of bed and straightened the duvet. While she had been talking on the phone, she suddenly realised she had been sleeping in Brett's bed. She had been too sleepy to notice before, but now she saw the masculine attire on the back of the chair, and the brushes on the dressing table. Guiltily, she collected her things together, feeling embarrassed even though Brett would never know.

As she walked towards the door, her

eye fell on a collection of photographs on top of the chest of drawers. The first one she noticed was of herself, soon after they had become engaged. It was a large colour photo, specially commissioned . . . and then she realised they were all of her. He'd kept and framed every last one. For a moment she was stunned, then she hurriedly left the room, anxious not to be found prying. She didn't know exactly why she felt so guilty when Brett was many miles away, but she felt like an intruder in his room.

Feeling decidedly hungry, she went to investigate the kitchen. She knew Brett had arranged for someone to restock the fridge, and sure enough she found fresh milk, bread and eggs. She set about making herself some breakfast, idly wondering how Brett coped on his own. At the Grange, they'd always employed staff to cook and clean. She didn't think he would have known how to boil an egg four years ago.

By the time she had consumed a

plate of scrambled egg and several slices of toast, she was beginning to feel more human; and after washing up, she wandered round the bungalow, being more observant this time. The kitchen was beautifully neat and tidy, with all the modern gadgets imaginable. She rather envied Brett his kitchen compared to hers at Primrose Cottage. She made a mental note that she really must do something about it when she returned home — if she decided to stay. There was still some doubt in her mind about that. It would depend on what Brett had to say.

The lounge looked functional but basic — it lacked a woman's touch, she said smugly to herself. There were no ornaments or cushions, no flowers or pictures — bar one. A framed picture of Fern hung over the fireplace and drew her attention immediately. So! Fern was the 'personal reason'. Her mouth went dry when she wondered what sort of hold she had over Brett. How had she come between them? Brett had never mentioned knowing anyone in America when they were courting.

Robina wondered whether she should stay after all. Now she had recovered from the travelling, she was beginning to have doubts about the wisdom of being there. In England it had seemed sensible, but now . . . Collecting a coat, she went to have a look outside. Maybe she should have a quick exploration of the market garden and then leave. She would have fulfilled her obligation, at any rate. Perhaps she could explore a little of the surrounding area; apparently, it was particularly scenic, according to the taxi driver. Maybe she could find a cheapish hotel to stay in.

It was raining, she discovered. Fine, gentle drizzle, but not cold; so, putting up the hood of her coat, she strolled towards the greenhouses. She wasn't feeling very amiable after having seen the picture — but, in a way, curious and perplexed. Her thoughts were once again troubled.

'Can I help you?' An elderly man

who was potting up some plants just inside the door accosted her.

'No, thanks. I'm just browsing.'

The man carried on with his work and Robina continued along the length of the greenhouse, taking a casual interest in the plants on display. As she passed the man on the way back, he looked at her quizzically.

'You're English aren't you?'

Robina smiled. 'How could you tell?'

'It's nice to hear the mother tongue,' he replied. 'You also have the look of an English rose about you.'

'Are you English, then?' she asked, smiling at his gentle flattery.

'Half-English, half-Scottish, but it's many a long year since I was back in the old country.'

'Where did you come from originally?' she asked, examining a tray of cuttings.

'A little place just outside London, although my father was from the Highlands of Scotland. My mother was English. Are you staying over here long?'

'I don't think so.' She moved on. 'Only until the owner arrives.'

'Friend of Brett's, are you?'

'Sort of,' she muttered, not wishing to disclose her association with Brett to one of his employees.

'Let me show you round, then. Brett would never forgive me if I let you escape without the full guided tour. I'm Charles, by the way. I'm in charge while he's away.'

'Robina,' she replied, shaking his grubby hand. 'I wouldn't want to take you away from your work.'

'No problem. There's always something to do in a place this size, but it's pleasant to take time off occasionally and see it through others' eyes. That's the way we get ideas of ways to expand.'

Charles was charming. Robina envisaged him as a gentleman of the old school with perfect manners: he treated her with exceptional courtesy. She was quite knowledgeable herself, but there were many plants peculiar to the area that fascinated her. The plot

229

was extensive and tidily maintained, although Robina didn't see many employees. Charles informed her they engaged extra staff when necessary — particularly at weekends when it got exceedingly busy.

The last part of the garden they came to was given over to roses. They grew in a profusion of every variety possible, but the one plot that captured Robina's whole attention and admiration was devoted simply to yellow ones. Charles silently watched her reaction, crinkling his eyes with understanding.

'They're special. All Brett's own handiwork. He won't let anyone else near them usually. He fusses over them something chronic. I doubt if a greenfly has the nerve to even think about landing there. Woe betide me if anything happens to them while he's away.'

Robina stared at the flowers as tears of joy sprang up. The flowers said so much — they were a labour of love — Brett's love for her . . . but why there?

She had never seen such a display.

Charles took out his secateurs and cut her a long-stemmed rose, still in bud but almost ready to open, and handed it to her.

'They're beautiful,' she said quietly. 'Thank you,' she added, as they once more walked back to the greenhouses.

Charles, she learned, had had a chequered career as a travelling salesman, car valeter, waiter, motel manager, and other less appealing jobs, he said — anything to keep body and soul together. That all changed when he met Brett, and together they had worked at making the garden the best in the district. They now had contracts to supply many of the leading hotels in the area, and they were getting their name spread far and wide.

It was nearly lunchtime when they finally parted company, and Robina returned to the bungalow feeling relaxed and content. It had been pleasant talking to Charles and hearing how Brett had turned what had been a run-down plot into a profit-making business. She wished she knew why he had chosen to travel so far away from Little Prestbury to do it, though. Charles obviously admired Brett very much: he'd praised him continually as they walked the full circuit of the market garden, stopping every so often to reposition a plant or to remark that something needed attention.

It was only when Robina saw the picture again that her resentment resurfaced. *May as well stay a bit longer,* she thought — *give it another day, at any rate.* Greg had given her his phone number in New York, but she didn't want to get in touch with him unless it was absolutely necessary, and he was the only other person she knew in America. For a start, she didn't want to come between him and his wife while he was trying for a reconciliation; and she also wanted to stand on her own two feet for a change. It was between her and Brett — or so she thought.

During the afternoon, she went into town. Charles had told her there was a convenient bus service she could use. It passed the entrance to the market garden on the hour. It had stopped raining by then, so she spent a leisurely couple of hours wandering round exploring the main department store, then the many bookshops and boutiques. It still felt strange being in a foreign country on her own, but she found she enjoyed herself.

While she was in town, Robina bought a newspaper and idly read the headlines as she sat on the bus on the way back to the bungalow. Suddenly she sat bolt upright. '*Final parting of the ways?*' it said, above a picture of herself and Greg at the airport, but when she read the column she realised they had totally misconstrued the situation. They had her down as a new companion for Greg, and the parting of the ways referred to Greg and Melissa.

Robina flushed with anger at the way she had been made to look like a marriage-breaker. She hurried back to the bungalow, not wanting to be seen by anyone. She did wonder about telephoning Greg, but decided not to — he would no doubt have already seen the article. What could she say, anyway? Greg was quite capable of riding out such notoriety — he was used to it.

She settled down to watch television as a means of trying to distract herself from worrying, but soon grew tired of it. She was making herself a meal when there was a knock at the door.

'Who is it?' she called warily.

'I don't know if you remember me — Fern.'

Biting back a sharp retort, Robina opened the door. Fern was the last person she wished to see. The girl stood uneasily in the porch, dressed in jeans and T-shirt. She looked much younger now, casually dressed and without the glamorous make-up she'd had on previously.

'Sorry to bother you if you're in the middle of something,' she said sulkily, 'but my father asked me to call. He thought you might be lonely.'

'Your father?' Robina queried.

'Stepfather, actually. You met him this morning in the greenhouse.'

'Oh — Charles, you mean.'

The girl looked furtive somehow.

'Thank him for his thoughtfulness, but tell him I'm fine.'

'Are you short of anything?'

'Not that I know of,' Robina said, quickly glancing at the pan of rice that was in danger of boiling over. She didn't wish to be rude, but had no desire for the woman's company.

Fern shrugged her shoulders and sauntered off, leaving Robina wondering just why she had come. Was it to see if she was alone? Had they seen the papers, and were they wondering if Greg was staying there? Or had Fern expected to find Brett home, maybe? Was she angry to find Robina staying in Brett's bungalow?

Robina unpacked her case in the spare bedroom and had an early night in bed — not that she thought she would sleep. She had far too much on her mind to hope for that. It seemed as if everyone she came in contact with was trying to mislead her — or was she being too suspicious? Perhaps Charles had sent his stepdaughter over simply out of concern for her wellbeing. Finally, she dropped into a fitful sleep.

9

Robina dreamt she was in an English country garden. She wore a white cotton sundress that buttoned right down the front. She recognised it as one of her favourites. It was full-skirted and decorated with lace panels and attractive pearl buttons. She had on a wide-brimmed sunhat trimmed with blue ribbon — a hat that Brett had bought for her on a visit to the seaside, so it was very precious to her. It was summertime; one of those hazy, lazy summer evenings when she could smell the wonderful scent of roses and new-mown hay. It was a sadly overgrown garden she was in, but she saw it as an exciting challenge. The waist-high grass was full of weeds, and the hedge shaggy and unkempt — but a haven for wildlife.

There was a small white-walled

cottage too, covered in honeysuckle and rambler roses. It also was in need of renovation. The paintwork was peeling and cobwebs festooned the windows, but she thought how charming it was going to be with a lot of love and some hard work. Robina was on a swing — a creaking, rusty swing, hung from a low branch of an old apple tree. Brett was pushing her higher and higher, and laughing at her girlish squeals. Then she fell. She was flying through the air, too far away for Brett to catch her. For a moment, she lay in a daze. She was on her back, staring up at the clear blue sky overhead. All around her was so quiet, just the crickets in the long grass and bees droning as they buzzed from flower to flower. Somewhere, far away, she heard a tractor chugging through the fields, and sheep calling plaintively — a typical summer's evening, in fact.

Brett came rushing over to her, anxiously asking if she was all right, his face deathly pale beneath the suntan. 'Are you all right, sweetheart? Anything damaged? Anything broken?'

She smiled mischievously. Instead of answering, she pulled him down so that she could kiss him. 'Only my heart; I seem to have lost it. Does that count?'

'Maybe we should check you out to make certain.' His voice changed markedly to a low, seductive undertone. 'You shouldn't be moved until we make absolutely certain that there is no damage. I read that somewhere. Just lie still.'

She felt him easing off her sandals and kissing her toes as his fingers gently massaged her feet. She giggled. Then his hands moved higher — smoothly up her bare, suntanned legs to rest on her thighs. 'No damage so far, all in immaculate condition. Such gorgeous, shapely legs you have.' Slowly, teasingly, he unbuttoned her dress and buried his head against her. 'I can hear your heart beating furiously. That's where the trouble is. What can we do about that?'

'What do you recommend, kind sir?' she replied softly, her hands finding their way inside his shirt.

'I just might have the very remedy.' He reached up to kiss her, at first softly, lingeringly while his hands sensuously explored her body at random. 'Rosie, Rosie my love. I can't wait for you to become my wife. We'll be so happy won't we? I can't believe how I've become so captivated and enslaved by such a sweet, innocent, young woman. I'll always take care of you, my darling. You are the love of my life.'

She remembered reading somewhere that one was nearer to God in a garden than anywhere else on earth. Well, she was in heaven. Bells were ringing, the sun was shining and the exquisite fragrance of roses filled the air.

★   ★   ★

She woke to see the one yellow rose in the vase by her bedside that Charles had given her, now opened up to show its true beauty. She rolled over and hugged the pillow, recalling her dream, and then with a sigh struggled out of bed. It was a dream she'd had so often. A dream that preceded the nightmare . . . and she didn't wish to be reminded of the nightmare. She tried her best to block out the memory of it by deliberately focusing her thoughts on mundane matters; but, as always, it was extremely difficult and almost impossible.

It was a warm, sunny morning, so after breakfast she found a deck chair and sat outside with a paperback to read. An enormous black-and-white cat came to keep her company, but otherwise she was left undisturbed. By lunchtime she hadn't read much of the book, but had spent most of the morning cogitating over what Brett was going to tell her when he came. She had thought and thought, but couldn't come up with any sensible solution.

She decided she would stay — at least until he arrived. Somehow she had no inclination to stir far from the bungalow. Apart from the notoriety the press had caused, she rather liked the closeness she felt to Brett while she was there. She could feel his presence in the house and could see why he was proud of it all. The business looked to be well-run and immaculately tidy — not that she had seen the books as anything to go by: it was more a feel for the place. If Fern hadn't put in an appearance, Robina might have been quietly content, but somehow the girl undermined all that. Fern obviously had some connection with Brett. Why else did he have her picture on the wall? Why else had she been asked to stay at Prestbury Grange?

Only Charles made contact with her. He called each day and asked if there was anything she needed, in a courteous manner, and seemed genuinely wishing to please. On the second day of her visit, he asked her out for a meal.

'Fern is going out, and I wondered if you would care to join me? I know a charming place in town if you like

Chinese cooking.'

Robina smiled at his kindness and accepted, mainly because she didn't want to hurt his feelings. He had been so polite and friendly. Charles called for her after the market garden closed and they drove into town in the firm's pick-up truck. It was a warm evening and she wore the blue dress she'd worn on her birthday. For some reason it seemed appropriate. He parked in a side street, and as they walked the short distance to the café, Charles greeted many passers-by.

'You seem very well-known around here,' she observed. 'Have you lived here long?'

'Close on six years, I guess. I settled here when I married my wife Lottie. It's the longest I've stayed anywhere. I've been a bit of a rolling stone for most of my life, but when I met her I knew I had found my soul mate. She's made me into a reformed character and I don't know what I would do without her now.'

He guided her into a small establishment just off the main street, and introduced her to the owner. They were given a pleasant table and made most welcome.

'How long have you known Brett?' Charles opened the conversation once their order had been taken.

Robina realised Charles must be curious about their relationship. She had come hundreds of miles to stay at his house after all, and yet she still felt reticent about saying much.

'I suppose you could say nearly all my life,' she said, 'but that is not strictly true. We lived in the same village, and I knew of him, but it was only when I reached my teens we became acquainted. We met by accident when my bike got a puncture. I was walking back along the road when Brett came by in his car and offered me a lift. He was like a knight in shining armour, I thought, with his dashing good looks and super sports car. All the girls in the village raved over him. Anyway, he was awfully kind, and instead of just transporting me, he actually squeezed the bike in too and drove back to the Grange where he lived. There, he repaired the puncture for me himself, and asked me out for a date.'

'Hmm, that sounds like Brett. Always ready to help a damsel in distress.'

'You know him quite well then?'

'We go back a long time,' Charles said, but before he could say more their food arrived and the conversation reverted to the market garden and the area generally. Robina was pleased in a way, because she didn't feel like explaining further about her involvement with Brett to a stranger, even one as nice as Charles. She would have liked to have heard, however, how he and Brett had first met.

Charles told her how pleased he was that he had managed to increase the turnover while Brett had been away. He was looking forward to boasting to him about it when he returned. All in all, it was a very enjoyable evening; and

Charles dropped her off at Brett's house at ten o'clock, bidding her a pleasant goodnight, and thanking her for her company.

★ ★ ★

The next morning Robina slept late and was woken by a loud knocking at the door. Quickly throwing on a dressing gown she went to answer it, fearful there had been trouble of some sort. Charles had told her they did occasionally get vandals paying them a visit, but it wasn't often, thank goodness because they were some distance from town.

She opened the door cautiously, but was taken by surprise to see Greg on the doorstep.

'Robbie. So I have got the right place.'

'What are you doing here?' she asked, glancing past him to see if Charles was about.

'Looking for you, of course. I

246

wondered if you saw the splash in the tabloids the other day? I hoped if you had seen it that it hadn't upset you too much.'

'You'd best come in.' Robina pulled her dressing gown cord tightly round her and led the way into the kitchen. She filled the kettle and switched it on.

'I'm sorry, Greg. I didn't pay any attention to the photographers at the airport. I thought they were only photographing you. I didn't realise they snapped me along with you. What happened when you went to see Melissa? Surely she understood? You said she didn't pay attention to what reporters said.'

Greg pulled out a chair and sat down. He looked shattered. 'Melissa was in a flaming temper and flung a newspaper at me the minute I walked in the door. She asked if I'd taken leave of my senses, going about with someone young enough to be my daughter. She didn't give me time to explain. She wasn't in a mood to listen to anything I said.'

'Oh dear, I am sorry. I didn't know the photographers would be waiting at the airport waiting to pounce like that. It's not something I'm used to. Did someone send her the papers from back home too?'

He nodded wearily.

'I'm sorry for all the bother I've caused,' she continued, 'but you should have told me. We could have left the airport separately if I'd known. It's all a mess, isn't it?'

'It wasn't you, my pet. Melissa would have found some other excuse to rant and rave at me, so if the press hadn't done their stuff it would have been something or someone else. She's found herself some dashing young gigolo and wants her freedom. I suppose it is only what I've been expecting. I've been deluding myself this last summer. I heard rumours . . . there are always rumours in our profession . . . but never mind — that's life, as they say.' He looked at Robina wistfully. 'We've had some great times this last summer, though, haven't we? I thought absence was supposed to make the heart grow fonder — but not, it appears, where Melissa is concerned.'

'Oh Greg, I am sorry. What can I do to help? Would you like me to go and see her and explain? Have you had breakfast, by the way? You look exhausted.'

'No. I didn't stop en route. I've been wondering how you were getting on. I've been tied up with producers for a couple of days, then I came straight here thinking I'd better warn you that Melissa might just give the press this address if she's feeling particularly vindictive.'

'Oh gosh, what can I do? Brett will be here soon and I promised to stay.'

'I think better on a full stomach.' He grinned. 'Can I make myself useful?'

Robina immediately set about cooking eggs and bacon while he made the coffee. They were sitting companionably at the kitchen table debating what they should do next when the back door flew open and Brett walked in. There was deadly silence as they all stared at each other in surprise.

'What the devil . . . ?'

'Why didn't you . . . ?'

'I can explain . . . '

They all spoke at once. Robina was suddenly conscious of how her dressing gown opened revealingly at the neckline, and guessed what Brett would be thinking.

He slung his overnight bag over his shoulder and, without another word, walked straight through the kitchen, glaring bleakly at Robina in passing, and slammed the door on his way into the hall.

'I'd best go and explain,' she whispered.

'I don't somehow think he's in any mood for explanations, love. I'm afraid it rather looks as if we've dropped another clanger.'

'But there's nothing clandestine about this situation,' she contested vigorously.

'Try to see it from his viewpoint, Robbie. It must look awfully suspicious, you and me sitting here in his kitchen at this time of morning. I'd best go. Maybe you can salvage something from all this if I leave. I don't want to mess up your life as well as my own. You've still got my number in New York, so if there's a problem, ring me there and let me know, OK?'

Robina saw Greg drive away and then went into the hallway. She listened for a moment to find out where Brett was. The slamming and banging came from his bedroom. He sounded almost berserk. Quickly, she dived into her own room and pulled on a pair of jeans and a sweater. She decided she would have to make her escape before Brett reappeared. He didn't sound to be in any mood to heed any apology or excuse. Greg was right: he would need time to cool off. He'd obviously made up his mind about what he'd seen. She wished now she had got a lift with Greg. She hadn't been

251

thinking straight.

Robina threw clothes into her case, collected her anorak from the peg and her bag from the chair, then rushed out of the door. She was almost sobbing with hysteria, cursing at the way everything seemed to go wrong, and how easily one could be misjudged. Why couldn't people wait to hear both sides before making up their minds? she thought angrily. She ran down the path, hoping to catch a bus into town. In her haste, however, she found she had taken the wrong route past the greenhouses. Turning abruptly to retrace her steps, she slipped and fell full-length on a wet slippery patch that she hadn't noticed. Her case went flying, demolishing some plant pots, sending them clattering to the ground.

Charles heard the commotion and ran to see what was going on. He helped her to her feet, greatly concerned. 'Are you all right, Robbie?' he asked, leading her over to a bench near the shed where he had been working. 'I thought it was that confounded cat again. I was ready to turn the hosepipe on it.'

She hobbled uncomfortably. 'Damn. I think I've sprained my ankle. I'm sorry about the plants. Please, Charles, will you call me a taxi? I need to get away.'

'A taxi?' he queried. 'I thought . . . '

'Please,' she urged, more concerned about getting clean away than with the state of her ankle. 'I can't stay here. He's furious with me. I should never have come. I knew it was a mistake from the very beginning.'

'Now, then. Calm down and tell me what's happened. I guess Brett is home. He would never harm you though, Robbie. It's me he'd like to murder. I'm the cause of all the unhappiness between you. I'll sort this out . . . '

'No, Charles. He thinks . . . ' Robina had grown quite fond of the calm, elderly man with his quiet dignity. She felt she could tell him her troubles and he would understand — he wouldn't jump to conclusions like others did. Before she got a chance to tell him though, she heard the back door of the bungalow slam and the next minute Brett stormed over.

'I thought we agreed you would stay away from her and let me handle it my way!' He glowered at Charles.

'Good morning, Brett. Welcome back,' Charles said quietly. 'You decreed so, maybe, but I wanted Robbie to get to know me as I am now, before she hears all the sordid details. She's a sensible girl with a mind of her own, and I didn't want her prejudiced. I haven't told her anything, if that's what's bothering you. She needs help now anyway, as she's twisted her ankle; so before you go off at the deep end, perhaps it would be best to see to that first.'

Charles patted Robina's hand sympathetically. 'I'll see you later, my dear. Don't let him bully you. He doesn't mean to upset you. Don't go haring off back to England — at least not before saying good-bye, will you?' Then, turning to Brett again, he said, 'I'd like a chance to put my side of the picture later, if I may? If we are still on speaking terms, that is. How about you both come over for dinner? Lottie's coming home today, and she would like to meet Robbie.'

Robina gazed from one to the other; they glowered as if preparing for a fight. At that moment, they looked alike, albeit Charles was considerably older and his hair was almost white. She didn't know what to make of the conversation.

Brett suddenly sagged. 'I suppose you're right. I guess I overreacted. I'm bushed. I'll let you know about dinner if you don't mind. I have other things to sort out first.' He bent to pluck Robina off the bench before she realised what he intended, and marched back to the bungalow without another word. She was so bewildered that she didn't know what to say.

'It was . . . '

'Later, love. Let's get inside first, huh?'

He strode purposefully through into the lounge and set her down on the settee. With infinite care, he removed her shoes to examine her ankles.

'Does it hurt?' he asked as he manipulated each in turn.

What could she say? Her heart was beating feverishly and she couldn't think beyond the pain in her chest. She winced when he put pressure on her left ankle.

'Hmm. Found a sensitive spot, have I? We'll fix you up in a jiffy.' He turned towards the door, and stopped mid-stride, swearing profusely. 'I'll wring that girl's neck if it's the last thing I do!' he growled and stormed out. Robina heard him open the back door and shout for Scottie — the employees' name for Charles.

'Where's that delinquent young madam?'

'I presume you mean Fern. I believe she's working at the far end of the garden. Shall I fetch her?'

'Yes,' he said tersely, 'and tell her to pad her backside, too.'

Robina stayed where she was, not daring to move. She had never seen Brett so angry, and she feared she may be the next target for his disapproval. She wondered what Fern had done to upset him. She certainly wouldn't want to be in her shoes, from the sound of it.

Brett arrived back with some ice cubes wrapped in a towel, and an elastic bandage. He proceeded to make her foot comfortable, and had just completed the task when Fern slunk into the room.

'I didn't know you were back,' she said, gulping nervously. The poor girl looked terrified. Her gaze went from Brett to Robina, and then slid over to the picture over the mantelpiece.

'Naturally,' Brett said sarcastically. 'Now explain yourself.'

'What?' she asked, hopping from one foot to the other.

'You know jolly well what. That!' he said tersely, pointing to the picture. 'I'll

257

give you ten seconds to take it down and put back the one that should be there.

'Coffee?' he asked Robina.

She nodded mutely.

When Brett left the room, Fern ran to remove the offending picture, glaring mutinously at Robina as if it was all her fault. She hurriedly unearthed another one about the same size from a drawer in the sideboard. This, she hung in its place, and then scurried away as her tears gathered momentum.

Robina stared at the replacement. It was an oil painting of herself — one that she'd never seen, and certainly never done a sitting for. It was the focus of the room, too. Positioned as it was, it drew one's eyes instinctively, just as Fern's had.

'Like it?' Brett asked, quietly entering the doorway with the beakers of coffee. 'I had it done from photos. It's not a bad likeness, I think, although not as good as the real thing. The eyes aren't quite right.'

Robina swallowed as tears prickled her eyes. His love and devotion shone like a beacon everywhere. How could she have been so blind?

'Like I told you, Rosie, I could never forget you, my love. Nor did I ever want to. It was unfortunate circumstances that parted us. Here, drink your coffee.'

'I know how it must have looked to you, seeing Greg in your kitchen at that time of the morning,' Robina said quietly. 'It looks as if his marriage is over. He'd just arrived, having driven all night, and I was only giving him breakfast. There has never been anything between us apart from friendship.'

'I know. I was so keyed up, though — looking forward to seeing you. Feeling apprehensive, too, hoping you would still be here. He was the last person I wished to see in my house when I arrived.'

'I didn't invite him. It was all perfectly innocent.'

'I realise that. I just don't like the fellow, that's all. Anyway, he's gone now. We can forget about him.'

'Please, Brett,' she said as he sat down next to her. 'Tell me what's been going on. I'm tired of all the mystery and uncertainty. What did Charles mean when he said *he* was the cause of our trouble? I don't understand. How could . . . ?'

'All in good time.'

Placing his beaker down, and before she realised what he was doing, he caught hold of her hand and slipped the engagement ring back onto it.

She gazed at the ring and then looked up at him questioningly.

'I'm going to assume, since you came here at my request and you decided to stay, even though you could have left at any time, that you have gone some way towards forgiving me. Now, I'd like to convince you that I love you, I've always loved you, I've never stopped loving you, and will do so for the rest of my life, no matter what the outcome. I'd like first to clear up one of your doubts.' He pulled her into the shelter of his arms and she could feel his heart thumping next to her own. 'Do you remember,' he said softly, 'the time you hurt yourself when you fell off the swing? It was the last time I saw you before my hasty departure.'

She nodded, blushing slightly.

'I think I'll have to repeat the remedy like before, and then maybe you'll accept what I say. You are the love of my life, Robina Rosaline Davison. You are the only one to fire me with such desire that simply overwhelms my senses. You, my dearest, are the most incredibly sexy lady I could ever wish to meet. How you could possibly think you couldn't please a man defeats me. All I can say is I only hope that you can be satisfied with me.'

'Satisfied?' she queried, with a mocking grin. Something of the old Brett showed, though not quite so brash as in the old days.

'Grr. You young monkey. I'm going to lock the doors, take the phone off the hook and I'll not let you escape from these four walls until I've convinced you of my complete and utter devotion.

I want to see those eyes sparkling like sapphires again, full of tender, sincere love, and not because they are overflowing with tears. I want to show you how very special you are to me, my sweet, adorable Rosie. Oh, how I've missed your warmth and companionship, your delightful simplicity, and your complete and utter adoration.'

Putting his words into action, he collected the beakers, and she heard him go to both outside doors, then the sound of the locks snecking. She stayed on the settee, excitement mounting. Obviously he was going to spin out his confession as long as possible, but she didn't care now. She was curious but not anxious about what had happened. Everything was going to turn out all right, she felt certain. He looked so confident, and she rather liked the masterful way he spoke. This was like the Brett of old. She didn't want to say anything that might upset things. Not now.

'Come, my little rosebud. I'm tired.

I've had a long flight, I've not slept for what seems like weeks and I need my beauty sleep, but I'm not letting you out of my sight for a minute.' Scooping her up into his arms, he strode into his bedroom and nudged the door shut behind them. Setting her down on the bed, he looked at her questioningly. 'I expected a protest. I thought you'd be outraged. Do you trust me, then?'

'If you can mend my broken heart, I'll certainly not protest,' she whispered, looking at him with heartfelt devotion. 'I'm confused by all the mystery, but I've always trusted you, Brett. I love you and I always will.'

'Oh, my love. How I've yearned to hear you saying those words to me again.' Pulling her into his arms, he kissed her passionately . . .

★　★　★

'Now do you believe me?' Brett murmured, afterwards, as he fell into blissful sleep.

Robina gazed at his face, now softened and relaxed, wondering what his story could possibly be, whenever he got round to tell it. What had produced the lines of worry? She lay beside him for a long time, happy to be with him and wearing his ring once more. He wanted them to start the family they'd planned! If that was the case, then she couldn't agree more.

She was about to get out of bed when his hand slid round her, pulling her back.

'Where do you think you are going?'

She snuggled back again.

'Nowhere, sweetheart. I'm staying right here with you.'

10

They both slept. It was early afternoon when Robina stirred. She had cramp in her foot. In the process of cautiously waggling it around, she woke Brett.

'Are you OK?' he asked, pulling her into his arms.

'Fine,' she whispered, and chuckled. 'I like your remedies.'

He grinned. 'Thank goodness for that. I suppose now I'd better confess all, since I've convinced you that you'll have to marry me.'

'Pretty sure of yourself, weren't you? Besides, I don't believe you said anything about marriage. I haven't agreed . . . '

'Do you want convincing further?' He kissed her neck fervently, tickling her with his hair, until she cried out for mercy and laughingly asked him to stop.

'OK, I give in. I'll marry you.'

'I may have looked a bit macho, but underneath I was quaking with dread that you'd turn me down,' he said seriously. 'I remembered very clearly what you told me when I arrived in your office the day after the funeral, and the day you returned my ring.'

'I didn't really mean it on either occasion. I was upset and wanted to lash out at you.'

'You had every right be angry with me, it's only what I expected. I was miserable, to say the least, when I realised you had a boyfriend you were serious about. Then I met Susan one day in the village and discovered there was no boyfriend after all. I didn't know whether to be relieved or not, after what I'd put you through. Susan seemed to think that I was in with a chance, so I decided I had to come clean.

'Anyway, my confession. Sorry it took so long to get round to it. I wanted you to meet Charles first. I'm sorry I couldn't introduce you both personally, but I suppose you realise by now that he is my father. I assumed you would see the resemblance, and . . . well . . . if you were still here when I arrived, then you had accepted . . . '

She stared in amazement. 'Your father! I don't understand — what about . . . ?'

'Margaret and Gerald are in fact my aunt and uncle. Gerald is my father's elder brother.'

'When did you learn all this?'

'The night I jilted you,' he said quietly. 'It all came like a bolt out of the blue.'

'Go on,' she urged, sliding back into his arms.

'That night, I returned home on top of the world. I was feeling almost supersonic after the most incredible time of my life. Seduced by a chaste maiden in an overgrown rose garden!'

'Never! Did I really precipitate things? I wondered afterwards what your thoughts were. Whether you thought I was immoral for allowing it to happen. When I heard you'd left the next day, I felt sure it was because I had offended you in some way. It was my one and only experience, and I was terribly shy. I began to wonder if you thought I was salacious and wanton, or that I was plain hopeless at sex.'

Brett chuckled. 'I hope we have comprehensively scotched that particular thought. You are simply incredible, my love. I can't get enough of you. You distract me so much that I forget all else.'

'So what happened when you got home?' she asked, returning him to the topic they should be discussing.

Brett pulled a face, but continued with his disclosure. 'I had no inkling of the hammer blow that was about to fall. With hindsight, I could have done things differently, but that's neither here nor there. When I arrived back at the Grange after seeing you home, the folks were all looking flustered and grim-faced. I thought there must have been a death in the family or something.

'I was on a high, and when I breezed in and asked what was the matter they told me quite bluntly my father was in trouble again. I guess I must have looked somewhat mystified as you might expect, and looked at Gerald. My aunt rushed from the room in hysterics, and Marcus and Juliet were soon dispatched, leaving my uncle to explain. We sat in the library, I remember, and he related the whole story to me.

'Apparently, my mother died soon after I was born, and my father went to pieces. Rather than have me adopted, Gerald and Margaret took me in as a brother for Marcus, believing it was the honourable thing to do in the circum-stances, since they were the only close relatives. Mother apparently only had an older brother who was glad not to have the responsibility of taking care of me thrust upon him. Gerald declared my father had always been a misfit and a wanderer — never staying in one place long, and always in dire financial straits.

'According to him, he was totally unreliable and a disgrace to the family name, so I was taken into the household and became their child. No reference to my real father was ever made. At least, his name was never mentioned in the house to my knowledge. He was regarded as the black sheep of the Scott family, and told never to darken their doors again, no doubt.'

'Was Marcus aware of all this?'

'Yes, he knew, but Juliet didn't.'

'So what happened? Why did they tell you about him that night?'

'He was in trouble. He'd rung up in desperation asking for their help. He needed money urgently. He had married a widow with a teenage daughter, and for the first time in his life since my mother's death he was trying to settle down and provide for his family. He had been working on this market garden when it was put up for sale due to the death of its owner. A colleague suggested they bought it and ran it

270

between them. My father thought it a good idea since he'd just rented a house nearby, and he would probably have great difficulty in obtaining other work at his age.

'Without seeking any advice, they procured a sizeable loan at exorbitant repayment terms, and went into business. My father had no commercial aptitude, and was easily persuaded by his partner that it was a sound investment. It transpired that my father was to take care of looking after the stock, etcetera, leaving his partner to see to the financial side of the business. That proved to be a costly mistake. The partner landed them in big trouble — owing money all over the place, with not enough income to service it no matter how hard they tried. He was totally incompetent, and finally took his own life, which left my father with the burden of debt.

'My father needed money fast and asked Gerald for a loan until he could find a way out of his desperate situation. After all, they were brothers and it was only a loan he wanted, but Gerald wouldn't play ball. He said he'd had enough of pulling him out of one mess after another, so this time he wanted me to take on the responsibility. I suppose he thought I was taking after my father with my casual attitude to work, and it was time I learned a few harsh lessons.'

'Oh, Brett. That was unfair. Just because you weren't serious like Marcus didn't mean that you didn't work hard.'

'At the time, I was so bewildered by this turn of events, I packed a bag and headed for the airport. The tale my uncle told was so horrific, making me feel contemptible and worthless. I know I wasn't thinking straight, but I felt as if my whole life was a sham, and I had no idea of who I was any more. I spent most of the night and following morning sitting around waiting for a flight, in a complete daze. My whole world had been turned upside down in a matter of hours. I finally managed to get an unclaimed seat and flew out here, not knowing quite what to expect.

'I didn't anticipate being away long, Robbie. Just long enough to resolve my father's problems. I fully intended getting in touch with you once I'd got things sorted. I never meant to leave you like I did without a word. I know that was unforgivable, but I wasn't myself, you understand. As you can imagine, meeting my father for the first time at my age was daunting enough; but visiting him in prison was decidedly grim, I can tell you.'

'Gerald actually let his own brother go to prison rather than help him!' Robina said with disbelief.

'I don't suppose he did it deliberately. He probably didn't realise the seriousness of Dad's problems. Everything seemed to happen so fast. To cut a long story short, I managed to persuade Uncle Gerald to lend me some money to tide us over to meet the most pressing bills. With that and what I had saved already, we managed, and then I set about turning the business around. I couldn't just abandon my own father; and of course there was his wife Lottie — and also Fern, her daughter — to consider. I felt I had to stay and do what I could.'

'Of course you did. I can see that, but why on earth didn't you write and tell me, Brett? I could have helped too. I would have understood.'

'I wrote countless letters,' he said with a sigh, 'but tore every last one of them up. I couldn't face you — not after all that had happened. I wasn't who you thought I was. You believed I was the irrepressible, handsome Brett Scott of Prestbury Grange, not the son of a troublemaker and a layabout. You deserved better.'

'Charles is none of those, I am sure. He's charming, sensitive, and a perfect gentleman, if perhaps too easily led astray by others!'

'He has done his homework well with you hasn't he? You should hear the way Gerald goes on about him. You wouldn't think you were talking about the same person.'

'I always wondered why you were so different from Marcus. You must have inherited your more pleasing personality from your father. But I've always loved you, Brett, for who you are, not because you belonged to Prestbury Grange. That never interested me one little bit. I suppose when we first met, your family home and everything impressed me, but I'm not used to such a lifestyle, and I was looking forward to living in that little cottage once we were married. I would have understood if you'd told me. I'm rather saddened you thought I was only marrying you because you lived at the Grange. What sort of girl did you think I was?'

'Oh, Rosie, love, I knew you would have stuck by me. It was me that was confused and disoriented. I didn't know who I was. My self-confidence took a battering. By the time I'd sorted myself out, I thought it was too late to get in touch with you; besides which, I had nothing to offer.'

'It must have been quite a traumatic experience for Charles, being sent to jail, and for you to learn about him like that. So what have you been doing for the past four years, apart from making sure the business succeeds?'

'I've kept my nose to the grindstone as a means of trying to get over you. I could never forget you. I never ever wanted to, but to me you were unattainable. I was the son of a philanderer with obviously the same characteristics. Look what happened on our last evening together! I knew you wanted to save yourself for our wedding night. I took advantage of you.'

'Rubbish. We were engaged to be married, weren't we?'

'In any case, I couldn't ask you to put up with scrimping and scraping. I hadn't even a home to offer you. I put all my savings into the business. For a while, I lived with Dad and Lottie, but Fern made my life a complete misery, and how could I ask you to be involved with a man whom many thought of as a crook.'

'Your father is not a crook. I simply don't believe it. Oh, Brett, you should have written and told me everything. I loved you.'

'Loved?'

'I still do.' She grinned. 'Any moment away from you was torture.'

'I know, sweetheart — which made it all the more terrible. You were so young and innocent, I simply couldn't ask it of you. I couldn't involve you in my family's troubles. It wouldn't have been fair. After all, you were only seventeen years old at the time. Things were rather precarious for quite a long while. At one stage, I began to wonder if we would ever make a go of it. Gradually, however, we made progress, and we had some good fortune along the way. We managed to expand, and bought the adjoining plot of land, acquiring a tumbledown building along with it, which I renovated and turned into this bungalow in my spare time. I only finished it quite recently.

'At last, I had a home of my own and prospects, but by then I thought it was far too late; you would have got over me, so I thought it best to stay away. I didn't want to upset you further, and from the letters I received from home, I gathered you had a boyfriend. I don't suppose I would ever have plucked up courage to return to Little Prestbury if it hadn't been for Marcus's death. I couldn't bear seeing you out with other men, and yet I knew I had let you down badly.'

'Oh, Brett, as if I could ever forget you! We had such plans for the future, didn't we? I honestly thought you left because I had let you down in some way, and the only thing that sprang to mind was our lovemaking.'

'My darling, darling Rosie. You were my whole world. That night was the most wonderful, magical time I've ever experienced. Maybe I wasn't a very skilful lover. After all, events just took over. I never meant it to happen.'

'I was sure that was why you left. I was so inexperienced and shy. I wanted so much to please you.'

Brett hugged her close. 'I've been foolish and inconsiderate. I'm sorry, my love. You did say you were on the Pill, so I assumed you were prepared for what happened. It was only when I met Susan this summer, and she told me about your worries after I left, that I began to wonder.'

'You and Susan seem to have spent a good deal of time talking about me behind my back. I wonder what else she told you.' Robina bit her lip. 'I had finally plucked up courage and gone to see old Doc Morris that very morning about family planning. I was really embarrassed about going — he'd been our family doctor all my life — but he gave me a prescription and some fatherly advice. Obviously, I hadn't yet started taking the Pill that night, but I guess I didn't want to wait any longer. I didn't care if I got pregnant, I wanted you so badly. Then, when you left, I simply fell apart, my periods stopped, and I really thought ... Anyway, I wasn't. I was just ill.'

'I'm sorry I put you through all that, Rosie. Truly sorry.'

'It was my own fault. It was such a beautiful evening, and like you said, we got carried away. Anyway, what do you want to do now? Now that Marcus is dead I mean. What about the Grange?'

'That rather depends on you, my darling. This is all very difficult. As you know, I owe Gerald and Margaret a lot. They did after all bring me up and provided me with a good home and education. They meant well, even though in retrospect it would have been better for them to have told me about my father earlier. Now, of course, they need my help. They need someone to look after the estate. They had hoped that Juliet's husband would be able to cope with running it, but I rather doubt it. He's not used to that sort of business, and he doesn't like to get his hands dirty. He's just not cut out for it.'

'Would you like to go back to Little Prestbury in the circumstances?' Robina asked tentatively. 'After all you have built up here, could you happily return to the Grange and leave all this behind?'

'I truly want you to be happy, Rosie, and I promise I will abide by your decision, whatever it may be. I don't want to put any pressure on you, and you can take as long as you like to think it over. The question is: where would you like to live? We can stay here and expand the business; there's still plenty of scope for it. On the other hand, we could go back to England and live at the Grange. I might mention at this stage that if we go home, we would have the Grange to ourselves.

'My aunt and uncle have decided to retire to live in Spain now Juliet is married. The death of Marcus was the last straw, and the winters are proving too much for Aunt Margaret's rheumatism. They did consider selling up, but don't feel like rushing into burning their boats like that in case they don't take to living abroad. Besides which, it wouldn't be easy with the present state of the market.'

'I don't need any time to consider my answer.'

'That's a pity, because I rather like holding you captive. I could envisage days of bliss discussing options.'

She sat up and hugged her knees hoping what she had to confess wouldn't annoy him. 'I know what I would like to do. I do sincerely love what I see here. I think you have done a magnificent job. Please don't get me wrong, but I don't think I would truthfully want to live here permanently. I always wondered if I should have left the village ages ago and spread my wings, but I now realise I am a simple country girl at heart.

'If you really want to stay, then of course so would I, but I have the feeling you want to return to take over at the Grange; and if that is the case, then I'd love it too. I like Little Prestbury and all the familiar faces and places; I feel at home there. I hope I'm not disappointing you — I'm only trying to be honest about my feelings, but I want to be wherever you are. That's all I care about, whether it be in a tumbledown cottage or a mansion. I just want to be with you.'

Sitting up, Brett put an arm round her shoulders. 'You could never disappoint me, sweetheart. You have merely confirmed my first impression. So, what say we leave this business for my father to cope with? I'm sure that he's learned his lesson, and Lottie will make sure he stays on the straight and narrow from now on. It was through marrying her he settled down and went into business, and he's certainly stuck at it. He's a reformed character, by all accounts.'

'What about Fern?' Robina asked archly.

'Jealous?' he quizzed. 'Fern is Lottie's irrepressible daughter. Fern has made my life a misery, trailing around after me these last four years. She thinks she's in love with me. She went too far by replacing your painting with one of herself, though. She wants to become a model, and even followed me when I went home for the funeral, thinking I could get her into some fashion school or something.'

'How old is she?' Robina asked with a contented smile.

'Eighteen, would you believe? A precocious eighteen-year-old. Full of adolescent calf love.'

'I know how she feels, only she can't have you. You are spoken for.'

11

Charles opened the door of their house, welcoming them with a broad grin. 'All well?' he asked. 'Silly question. One only has to look at your contented faces to see that you've made up. Come along in and meet the missus. Lottie's dying to meet you.'

'I thought the others called you Scottie because you were of Scottish descent,' Robina said, handing him her coat. 'I didn't realise you were Brett's father. Although, now I come to look more closely, there is a family likeness.'

'Hmm. I rather hoped you wouldn't twig who I was, Robbie. Brett would have slaughtered me — and deservedly so — if you had run off before he returned. He wanted to do it all his own way, as usual. Do I take it there are no hard feelings? I really am terribly sorry for the trouble I've caused you two over the years through my own selfishness.'

'I don't see it was your fault entirely, Charles. I think Brett ought to have been told about you a long time ago. We all make mistakes from time to time, don't we? I know I have. In any event, if Brett had only written and explained, I would have understood. It was just not knowing that upset me. I began to think I wasn't good enough for him when he left without any explanation.'

'The boot was on the other foot, my love,' said Brett softly.

'I'm relieved you can be so understanding, Robbie. How's the ankle by the way?'

'Oh, it's fine. I just ricked it. It's no trouble.'

A plump, motherly woman emerged from the kitchen wiping her hands on her apron. 'Much prettier than the painting,' she said, smiling a welcome. 'I'm sorry I wasn't around when you first arrived. I've just got back from visiting my mother, who has been unwell.'

She ushered them into the sitting room. 'Fern has suddenly remembered an urgent appointment in town,' Lottie said with a shake of her head. 'I gather she's in the doghouse again. She's always up to some mischief or other, I'm afraid.'

'I expect she thinks it advisable to stay out of my way until I've calmed down,' Brett remarked with a wry grin. 'I must admit, I was pretty steamed up about her latest escapade.'

'Are we to deduce from the happy smiles that you two have resolved your differences?' Lottie said, looking anxiously from one to the other. 'No hard feelings?'

Brett put his arm round Robina's waist. 'I should have listened to your advice all along. You were both right, and I was wrong. Rosie says that no matter what's happened, she's still in love with me, and we are going to get married as soon as is practicable.'

'Well, congratulations to you both. We told him ages ago he should go and see you, my dear, but he was that stubborn . . . We were going to write to you ourselves once we knew what sacrifice he'd made, but unfortunately Fern overheard our plan and informed Brett. He refused to let us make contact with you. He'd heard you were going out with someone else and didn't want to interfere.'

'It was my way of trying to forget him, but it didn't work,' Robina said, smiling up at Brett. 'Nobody matched up to what I thought we had.'

'Some good has come out of Marcus's death, then. It's an ill wind, as they say. Now, make yourselves at home. Dinner is about ready,' Lottie said, preparing to return to the kitchen. 'I'll just dish up.'

'Can I help?' Robina volunteered. She warmed to the friendly, under-standing woman as she made her feel at ease in their comfortable home. Having seen Fern, she had been rather anxious about meeting her mother in case she was anything like her.

Lottie asked her to help carry the tureens on to the table so they could help themselves. 'Not knowing what your likes and dislikes were I thought it best. We don't stand on ceremony here. I'm so pleased you two have finally got together. Charles and I were both very upset when we realised what Brett had done. We felt guilty, but it appeared there was nothing we could do about it.'

Robina thanked her for their concern. 'It's strange, really, but I nearly didn't come. There was an accident onsite and Brett got hurt, and my father was worried he might sue us for negligence. Everyone kept telling me I needed a holiday, so when Brett asked me to come here, I thought it best to co-operate.'

The meal was simple but beautifully cooked and Charles and Lottie proved to be highly entertaining hosts. Charles even produced a bottle of champagne, which he said he'd put on ice as soon as he knew Robina was coming to stay.

They toasted the news of the engagement and imminent marriage.

Brett immediately told them of their decision. 'Now seems as good a time as any to let you know we have decided to return to Little Prestbury. Gerald needs someone to take charge and I'm the obvious man for the job.'

'So you'll trust me to look after the business here then, full time?' his father said. 'Aren't you taking quite a chance?'

'With a good woman at your side anything is possible. Rosie says she would live here if that was what I wanted, but in the circumstances I feel it best all round if we return home. I'm sure you'll be able to cope without me breathing down your neck. You have managed for the past few weeks, and I don't think it's any the worse from what I see — although I haven't inspected the books yet.'

'You might be interested to know the takings are up on the same month last year, and I have high hopes of selling plants to that new supermarket which has opened up at the other side of town. I managed to convince them it was worth a try, on a sale or return basis to start with.'

'Congratulations. We'll make a businessman of you yet. However, we do have one little problem to overcome. Rosie here is not quite such a pushover she used to be. At one time she would have done anything I asked without preconditions,' he chuckled. 'Now she declares she will only marry me if I agree to a wedding as originally planned at the village church in Little Prestbury, and also you are present too. She says she's proud to acknowledge you as my father and it is time everyone buried the hatchet. So what do you say, Dad? Do you feel up to facing the family and running the gauntlet of the village gossipmongers? You know what they're like — heaven knows what scandal they'll come up with about us.'

Charles looked slightly embarrassed. After clearing his throat and looking at Lottie he said, 'I'd be honoured and delighted to attend if that is your wish. I'm sure Robbie has had to put up with a lot already because of me, and if she wants everything out in the open then so be it. Lottie has never been to England, have you, love? You know, I think you're right, it is time I saw England again. I'm not sure what Gerald and Margaret will say though, but I'll be proud to attend my son's wedding.'

'I expect all families have some skeletons in the cupboards,' Robina said with a smile of understanding. 'I know I have some relatives who embarrass me, but you have done nothing to be ashamed of that I can see. And anyway I want our children to know their grandparents, so I hope you will visit us often. You might even think of returning to England to live some-time, maybe retire there — if you can persuade Lottie that it is. I know of a great little cottage . . . '

'Wherever did I get the impression you were a little mouse of a woman?' Brett said with a wicked grin.

★ ★ ★

At the church door two months later they paused for the photographs. Robina whispered to Brett that she hadn't known Greg was coming. She thought he was on location — which is what he'd told her.

Brett murmured, 'He'll do anything for publicity. Besides I thought he ought to be here, because he helped you through a very difficult patch, and provided the reason for me to plead my case. If it had been anyone else I might have gone back to America thinking you deserved to be happy if you had the chance. I wasn't going to interfere, but since it was him — a married man, that settled it as far as I was concerned. I had to press my case and see if there was the remotest chance for us.'

'I'm so glad you did,' she whispered and then gasped. 'Did you invite Melissa too? That is Melissa Holmes isn't it, surrounded by all those camera crews?'

He grinned. 'I believe Greg and Melissa are about to have a very public reconciliation. Smile sweetheart, the cameras are rolling. Think of it as a rehearsal for the various functions you'll have to attend — garden parties to give, fetes to open, etcetera. All expected as my wife, Mrs Brett Scott.'

She smiled. He was back — the Brett she knew of old.

We do hope that you have enjoyed reading this large print book.

Did you know that all of our titles are available for purchase?

We publish a wide range of high quality large print books including:
Romances, Mysteries, Classics
General Fiction
Non Fiction and Westerns

Special interest titles available in large print are:
The Little Oxford Dictionary
Music Book, Song Book
Hymn Book, Service Book

Also available from us courtesy of Oxford University Press:
Young Readers' Dictionary
(large print edition)
Young Readers' Thesaurus
(large print edition)

For further information or a free brochure, please contact us at:
Ulverscroft Large Print Books Ltd.,
The Green, Bradgate Road, Anstey,
Leicester, LE7 7FU, England.
Tel: (00 44) **0116 236 4325**
Fax: (00 44) **0116 234 0205**

Other titles in the
Linford Romance Library:

LADY EMMA'S REVENGE

Fenella J. Miller

Lady Emma Stanton is determined to discover who killed her husband, even if it means enlisting the assistance of a Bow Street Runner. Sergeant Samuel Ross is no gentleman; he has rough manners and little time for etiquette. So when Emma and Sam decide the best way to ferret out the criminal is to pose as husband and wife, they are quite the mismatched pair. Soon, each discovers they have growing feelings for the other — but an intimate relationship across such a social divide is out of the question . . .

STANDING THE TEST OF TIME

Sarah Purdue

When Grace Taylor wins a scholarship to study music at the exclusive Henry Tyndale School, she is determined to work hard to realise her dream of becoming a professional musician. There she meets the charming young Adam, and it feels like they were meant for each other — until a vicious bully with a wealthy father, to whom the school is beholden, succeeds in breaking them apart . . . Eight years later, fate throws Grace and Adam together again. Can they overcome the shadows of the past and make a life together?

EYE OF THE STORM

Sally Quilford

When Nadine Middleton travels to Egypt, she does not expect to meet Lancaster Smith, the man who discredited her father. As she embarks on a quest to clear Raleigh Middleton's name, she wonders who is friend and who is foe amongst the other passengers on the Nile steamer. With one apparent death and another person going missing, along with some mind-blowing and life-threatening riddles to solve, Nadine finds herself relying on Lancaster more and more — but can she trust him?